the Tree Keeper's Promise
-a novel-

OTHER BOOKS BY TAMARA PASSEY

The Christmas Tree Keeper: A Novel

Mothering through the Whirlwind

the Tree Keeper's Promise
-a novel-

TAMARA PASSEY

Winter Street Press

The Tree Keeper's Promise
Copyright © 2016 Tamara Passey
All Rights Reserved.

No portion of this work may be reproduced in print or electronically, other than brief excerpts for the purpose of reviews, without permission of the publisher.

This book is a work of fiction. All the characters, names, places, incidents, and dialogue in this novel are either products of the author's imagination or used fictitiously. Any resemblance to actual persons, places and events is coincidental.

Winter Street Press
winterstreetpress@gmail.com

Cover Design by Laura J. Miller 2016
www.anauthorsart.com

Library of Congress Control Number: 2016919143

ISBN-13: 978-0-9909840-3-0

1. Christmas–Fiction 2. Trees—Fiction 3. Miracles—Fiction

For Steve

PROLOGUE

Hans and Adeline Shafer, Sutton Massachusetts, 1881

The Planting

Taking her hand, he guided her to the edge of the land he'd cleared. The air around them stirred. The spring morning sun warmed their cheeks. He stopped at the newly-turned earth and gestured over it.

"See, your trees will grow. Our trees. And here is the soil from home." He held up the leather pouch. "I brought it for you to mix with this ground and these seeds."

"What good will it do?" she asked, pulling her hand away, grasping instead at her long braid. "The dirt here, the trees here. No one in this land wants the trees. They belong in Germany, meant to live and grow there. Like us. What can any of us do here?" She faced the horizon without showing any emotion, though one tear escaped her eye. Her hand rested on her growing belly.

"Adel, you know what these trees are. You know what they can do," he said, reaching for both of her hands, pleading for her blessing.

"You mean you planted the seeds of love?" she asked with wide eyes.

"That I did."

She took the pouch and gave it one shake over the upturned row by her feet.

"Hans, can they work here?" she asked, handing the pouch back to him.

"We shall see."

CHAPTER 1

They say no two trees are exactly alike. Growing them may be a science, but choosing the right one to decorate for Christmas—well, that's an art. And it was the only thing Angela's daughter wanted for her ninth birthday—to go to Mark Shafer's farm and find the perfect tree for Christmas. And why wouldn't she? As Mark's grandfather Papa Shafer had told them last year, they were miracle trees. It made no difference to her that it was only September. They could tie a ribbon around her choice and come back for it in December.

"Thank you," Angela whispered to Mark as they arrived at the section of trees designated for the upcoming season. "This will be her favorite birthday."

"I'm glad you asked," Mark said. "There was a time after you met my grandpa last year when I didn't think you'd ever want to come back," he said with a teasing grin.

Angela couldn't live down how annoyed she'd been about Papa's talk of miracle trees that first night. But he'd been right. And so much had changed since then, namely her heart.

"What can I say?" she said. "Papa won me over."

Well, *Mark* had won her over with his genuine eyes, his kind ways—and maybe his broad shoulders.

They walked down the path as it glowed in the afternoon sunlight. The crisp fall air surrounded them. This was much better than corralling a party of fourth-grade girls at the mall.

"Can this be the one for the farmhouse?" Caroline asked.

"We're here to pick out a tree for *our* house," Angela replied.

Papa chuckled. "That's fine with me. Seems like she's got an eye for this," he said as he walked closer to the tree she chose.

"You know, Mom, if you and Mark had made up your minds and gotten married, we wouldn't need to choose two trees."

"Caroline!" Angela's jaw dropped at her daughter's words. Though she knew Caroline didn't mean to embarrass her, there were lines better left uncrossed.

"Marriage isn't something to rush into," she said under her breath as she briefly met Mark's eyes.

A spark of humor crossed his face.

"The child's got a point," Papa said. "You two could make it official and call one place home."

"Not you too." Mark folded his arms over his chest.

As they continued their walk in the autumn sun, Mark reached for Angela's hand, something she hadn't grown tired of in the eight months they'd been dating.

Caroline ran ahead until she reached a certain tree. "Look at this one," Caroline said. "Lovely branches and such a presence."

Angela checked to see if Mark was also startled by the comment.

"What do you mean?" Angela asked as she watched Papa move to Caroline's side.

"Can't you see it? It's like this tree is determined to be noticed. Like you know Marie who does ballet? She looks official standing in the lunch line. How do you *not* notice her? Can't you tell there's something special about this one?"

Angela noticed the amused look on Mark's face and the serious one on Papa's. Her eyes narrowed on Caroline. Was she imitating what she'd heard Mark and Papa talk about, or was she actually seeing these traits, thinking this way about the trees?

"Special, is it? Do you want this one for your house?" Papa asked, moving close to the tree.

"Not now. Another year of growth, maybe two, and it will be just right," she said confidently as she moved on down the row.

At that, Mark reached up and scratched the back of his head.

"I've never seen anything quite like it," he muttered.

Angela asked, "Like what? This tree?"

"No, Caroline," Mark said.

Angela watched her daughter move along and touch the branches with her fingertips, Papa following close behind.

"Do you think she's making this up, maybe to impress Papa—or you?" Angela asked Mark.

He shook his head. "As strange as it sounds, I think she actually understands them."

"That's not so strange," Papa said, clearly having overheard Angela and Mark's conversation. "Some children are naturals. They're still full of light. No doubts."

Angela nodded. That certainly described her daughter.

"If you choose the right tree, Caroline, we could have a wedding around here. I'd say before Christmas," Papa said.

"What is that supposed to mean?" Angela asked with a little too much worry in her voice.

"It means Papa is losing patience with me," Mark answered.

"I'm not the one you need to worry about," Papa said and winked at Angela. "And it's more than that. Caroline, these trees here can make a love match. It doesn't happen very often, but when it does, it's a sweet kind of love."

"They can do *what*?" Mark asked, not hiding his surprise.

Papa answered quickly, "You heard me. A love match."

"Were you planning on telling *me* about this?" Mark asked, though Papa wasn't paying him much attention.

Angela could feel the heat burning in her cheeks, much the same way she did last year when she heard Papa say the trees could cause miracles. Though she didn't have trouble believing in miracles now, this was different. Wasn't it? She avoided eye contact with Mark, not sure she could trust even her eyebrows to behave.

A love match?

"I don't think the trees can have anything to do with wedding plans," Angela said casually but carefully.

"Maybe you're on to something," Mark said, stepping up to Papa and putting his arm around him. "Caroline, find a romantic looking tree for the farmhouse, could you? I bet Papa and Mrs. Shaw will be married in no time."

"That's a great idea." She laughed and ran even farther ahead.

"Nonsense," Papa said. "She isn't looking for a husband."

"How do you know?" Angela chimed in on the teasing, thankful Mark had shifted Papa's—and Caroline's—attention.

"She arrives at the farm early and leaves late. She's the independent kind. Never asks for help or company." Papa paused. "And she wears a lot of those cardigans."

"What do cardigans have to do with anything?" Mark asked.

Angela waited. Knowing Papa, he'd have a reason.

"Dark ones. Black, navy, gray."

"You think she's still in mourning?" Angela asked, incredulous. "Papa, her husband passed away over ten years ago."

"No, she doesn't wear them for grief. Those were her husband's favorite colors," Papa answered with a tone of defeat.

Angela stopped walking. Mark did too. Papa continued ahead of them.

"How does he know that?" Angela asked.

"How does Papa know anything? He just seems to know. It's a skill of his I've been trying to learn ever since I took ownership of the farm last year."

"Maybe he asked her," Angela said. Sure, her neighbor Mrs. Shaw had stepped in to run the craft barn after their family friend Donna had passed away. But Papa focused on weather patterns and planting strategies. Had he even noticed Mrs. Shaw?

"Do you think he's interested in her?"

Mark didn't answer. He reached for Angela's hand again.

"And what does he mean *love match*?" Angela asked. "Is he serious?"

"I've never known Papa to joke about the trees. If I've learned anything this year, it's that he takes them very seriously."

"Has he said anything like that before?"

A moment or two passed as Mark thought about it.

"Not directly, no. But he has mentioned love here and there."

Angela waited. "Go on."

"Oh, you know, he says 'The trees are all about love.'"

"But anything about love matches or couples? Weddings?"

Caroline interrupted. "Papa, Mom, look over here." She stood in front of a healthy Scotch pine as a breeze swirled around her hair and branches bobbed in the current. She gazed up at the top.

"I found it! This one is for our house." Caroline put her hands on her hips. "Can I have that ribbon now?"

Angela handed it to her and watched as she skillfully

maneuvered through the branches to the trunk. The ribbon wasn't quite long enough to fit around it and form a knot, so she used the base of a branch jutting out from the trunk and tied a double-knotted bow with the red-and-white polka-dot ribbon.

"There. Nice and tight," she said. "Now the tree for the farmhouse. Look over here."

Angela followed her while Mark and Papa stood talking, maybe about Caroline's choice of tree.

"What do you think of this one? It will be perfect in the front room of Mark's house. Too bad we couldn't put it up today so you and Mark could have a wedding soon."

Angela clenched her jaw.

"Do you think it can count if we just tag it?" Caroline asked.

"Listen, Papa is having a little fun with you today. I'm not so sure trees can make love matches."

"Sure they can. These are Shafer trees, remember? They cause miracles," Caroline said. "Remember how after we put up our tree last year, we paid the rent and you got a new job? And then we found the treasure on the farm with Mark?"

"Yes, but—"

"That's what I mean. So you've heard of the miracle of love, right?" Caroline continued.

Angela had no defense for that. Maybe a distraction would work. "I didn't bring another ribbon. We'll have to come out again."

Caroline stepped back and reached for her small ponytail. She pulled at the yellow sunflower ponytail holder until it was free and then worked it around one of the tree's short branches.

"There. That will do." Caroline sighed loudly.

"What was that for?" Angela asked, referring to her sigh.

"I still think we only need one tree."

"You mean you only *want* one tree," Angela clarified.

"Whatever. Wouldn't it be awesome to wake up Christmas morning at the farm and you and Mark could be married? That would be the present ever. I wouldn't need anything else."

Angela found herself picturing it, but only for a second before reality set in. "Caroline, Christmas is less than four months away."

Caroline shrugged. "Don't doubt the trees, Mom."

They walked back to the farmhouse, Caroline flitting between Angela and Mark, then catching up with Papa, who led the way.

"She believes him, you know. Love-match trees," Angela said to Mark. "Any idea how that's supposed to work?"

"None whatsoever. I'll ask him on our next walk." Mark brushed a strand of hair off her forehead. "Is that fear I see?"

Angela took a breath, then a deeper one, willing the furrow to disappear—at least enough that she wouldn't look petrified. A wedding before Christmas, and she and Mark weren't even engaged. She didn't fault him. In January, she'd opened her big mouth about "four seasons."

She'd told him about her mother's idea of knowing each other through four seasons before getting married—advice she'd given Angela the first time around. Advice she had ignored, of course. This time she thought she should try it out, and maybe avoid past mistakes.

It had been exciting when they'd found the treasure box together last Christmas Day, right where Mark's dad had told Angela's mom he'd put it some thirty years earlier. Yes, it was remarkable to find the seeds, a leather pouch, and a diamond band. But they'd hardly known each other then and had only been caught up in the thrill of the discovery. No matter how good it felt when Mark had put the ring on her finger, giving it back had been the right thing to do.

And no matter how much she liked it when he had kissed her, she would not rush into marriage this time. She would not have another fair-weather husband.

Mark hadn't argued with them taking their time. She actually didn't mean to say he couldn't propose until four seasons had passed, but here they were in September. Angela had wondered if Mark would propose on Christmas Day, maybe a little reenactment of last year, only this time without the audience and somewhere a little less dusty than the toolshed. And that would give her enough time to be sure she wasn't rushing into this relationship.

So why should she be worried about Papa's little comment?

Any potential proposal was months away. There would be no wedding before Christmas, no matter what tree Caroline chose.

CHAPTER 2

Mark moved through the darkened farmhouse and stepped on the floorboard closest to the wall—the one that didn't creak. The mid-September morning chill caused him to reach for his overcoat. But he changed his mind. *It'll warm up soon enough.*

He slipped out of the side door and strode over the gravel to Papa's cabin. Their walks had turned into training sessions this year. At first Papa had become more talkative and shared random things about the farm. Then Mark had noticed a pattern of systematic instruction: from soil mixtures to planting schedules to shearing techniques.

Usually Mark paid attention, but lately he'd been thinking of Angela and when he would propose, and how. He hadn't discussed any of this with his grandfather yet. Not that there was a problem. Papa and Angela got along well—but Mark liked giving Papa the impression that his focus wasn't divided. Like today, he wanted to know more about the trees, but he also couldn't stop thinking of Angela's curious reaction to Papa's declaration of love-match trees. Mark liked the idea of a wedding before Christmas, but Angela seemed bothered by it. He knew about her mother's four-seasons rule, but was there something else holding her back? Or was it the other way around? Was she frustrated that he hadn't proposed yet?

The last few weeks of morning walks with Papa had been quieter, leaving Mark with the impression that they'd reached the end of what his grandfather had to teach. Not that Mark wanted their walks to end, but maybe his time as student could be done.

Mark spotted Papa, lean and tough, sauntering down the path from the cabin, a deliberate strength in his step. Mark liked to think Papa would walk the farm forever that way.

"There you are," Papa said.

"Nice chill in the air. I almost wore my coat."

"Don't be fooled by it. We've got a warm spell coming our way yet," Papa said.

"What gives you that idea?"

Papa didn't answer right away. They covered a few more yards to the back lot of trees. Papa motioned to his right, where some of the new seedlings had been planted.

"Don't they look like they're ready for a growth spurt? Don't it look like they're gonna shoot up another inch or two when we're not looking?" Papa grinned as he stated this more than asked. "They wouldn't be looking that way if it weren't about to go warm on us."

Mark strained at the trees. They were seedlings and had fared well. They were growing, no doubt about it. But what did Papa mean? One minute Mark felt like he knew all he needed to know and that he could understand what Papa was talking about. And then there were moments like this one where clearly he was missing something.

Mark remembered what Papa had said the day before. "All this time we've spent together and you've never said anything to me about love matches," Mark said.

"That sounds about right."

"Why not?" he asked.

Papa didn't answer right away. "I don't recall you asking."

"Caroline didn't ask either. Are you sure you weren't making it up for her sake?"

Papa straightened his back and shook his head.

"I've told you before, I don't have to make things up when it comes to the trees."

Mark exhaled in frustration. "What else haven't you told me? I mean, I hear something like this and I wonder."

Papa remained quiet.

"I mean it, Papa."

"I can tell," Papa said.

"I need to know everything there is to know about the trees," Mark said. "No, I *want* to know everything about the trees." Mark stopped walking and held his hands out for emphasis.

"Well, it sounds like we can begin." Papa put his hands on his hips and took a step back from the row of trees.

"Begin?" Mark couldn't contain his exasperation. "Begin what?"

"Keeper training."

"How is that any different than what we've been doing all year? What have you been teaching me?"

"Ah, textbook stuff. Basics."

"And keeper training is more than that?" Mark shook his head.

Papa chuckled a soft, easy laugh. "You could say that. And you can't go finding it in a book."

Mark started walking again. He watched Papa keep pace and felt the funniest twinge in his stomach.

"Then I'm ready—as ready as I'll ever be."

"Good." Papa stopped at a tree, stood squarely in front of it, then stretched out one arm to meet a long branch. "The first thing you gotta keep in your mind at all times here on the lot, up there in the house, by yourself, or with customers . . ." Papa paused.

"I'm listening . . . by myself or with customers." Mark nodded to show he was paying attention.

"First thing to remember is love. It begins and ends with love here. The trees, the land, the house, the people. None of it would be ours if it weren't for love. The only way for the trees to keep growing is to make sure they are getting all the love they need."

The silence that followed was punctuated by a gust of wind.

Papa continued. "Love is growth. You know? Love creates. Love builds. Love gives life. If you let yourself think about it, you'll start to see what I mean."

"Okay, got it," Mark stated. He scanned the trees. "Love." That one word sobered him, caused him to square his shoulders. It was something he'd already been thinking about, playing a kind of mental tug-of-war with what it was—what it wasn't. And whether he loved someone in particular.

"Looks like you're wearin' a question on your face," Papa said. "Best to ask it now, before it hides behind your pride."

"How do you know if it's love?" The question clearly related to Mark's thoughts about Angela, not the trees. But Papa didn't seem to notice.

"You'll be there for them. You'll *want* to be there for them."

"Is it the same for people?" Mark ventured.

Papa smiled. "People are trickier. But I'd say they begin and end with love too. At least the lucky ones do."

Mark left Papa by the front lot of trees and walked casually around the farmhouse. On their next outing, Papa said they'd talk about timing—not planting schedules but how the trees would help him know when to make changes.

All this time and still more to learn.

Much like Papa, the farmhouse was starting to show its age but was still as strong and sturdy as ever. Mark passed the porch rails and noted they were in need of a new coat of paint. The roof shingles were looking weathered. He could take care of those things now that the room he'd added was almost done. He rounded the west side of the house and inspected the new wall. It had changed the angle of the walking path. Now customers needed to walk far out and around the farmhouse to get to Donna's craft barn. Yet, much to his surprise, the addition had turned out exactly the way he'd pictured it, so he didn't question the alterations.

Mark went inside and closed the office door. He surveyed the land from the window before sitting at his desk. *Love creates, love builds,* he thought. He opened the bottom desk drawer and pulled out a legal-sized file folder. Smoothing his hand over the architect's plans, he smiled at the anticipation he felt. It hadn't been easy to keep it a secret, but no one knew what the addition to the house was. Not Angela, not Brett, not Mrs. Shaw. Not even Papa. This was his surprise for Angela. He couldn't wait to show her what he'd built for her.

The door opened. Mark sat up, grabbed the file, and in one motion stashed it back in the drawer.

Papa walked in and sat on the other side of the desk.

"Didn't mean to disturb you."

Mark cleared his throat to respond, but Papa continued.

"Unless you're up to something I should know about, then I'm glad I found you," he paused. "Now that it's about done, are you gonna fess up? It looks like you've added a new wing, like we were the county hospital or something."

"It's not as big as that—and it's a surprise for Angela. Remember?" He was being vague, but it was the truth.

"Keeping secrets, are ya? Watch yourself. Secrets can backfire if you're not careful. Especially early on. It's best to surprise a girl after you've earned her trust. If you try surprising her before you have it—you may never get to earnin' it."

How did Papa do it? How did he *know* things? Mark didn't want to lose Angela's trust, but as he'd learned, timing could be everything.

"I suppose it's a big fancy bedroom you've added. Have you proposed?"

"Not yet."

"Just as well."

An extra bedroom would have made sense. But that wasn't what he'd done. And it probably wasn't a good idea to give Papa the wrong impression.

"It's not a bedroom," Mark said carefully.

"It's not?" Papa leaned forward on the edge of his chair. "Then I need to ask you about some new arrangements I'd like to make. What d'ya say we trade places? You give the cabin a try and I take the farmhouse for the season?"

Mark sat up straighter. Papa had never suggested anything like this, never even hinted at it. The cabin was small and primitive, but Papa had never complained. He'd moved into it after Nana died years ago, and it seemed to suit him fine. What could he want with the farmhouse? And why trade places?

"Papa, if you need more room than the cabin, just say the word. We can clean out the extra bedroom—Kate's things can go to the basement. Is there anything wrong with it?"

"You don't have to move your sister's things. And there's nothing wrong with the cabin. It's the perfect home for a single man," Papa said with a mischievous twinkle in his eye, then he sat back comfortably in his chair as if he had all the time in the world.

"What does that mean?" Mark asked.

As far as Mark could tell, they were both single men at the moment. And if either one of them had a hope of changing that status, it was Mark. *Wasn't it?*

"Means I'm planning to ask Mrs. Shaw to marry me, and I'm

predicting she'll say yes. The farmhouse will make a much better honeymoon suite than the cabin. Wouldn't you agree?"

Mark would agree if he weren't speechless. *Propose? Papa and Mrs. Shaw?* Sure they'd teased Papa about it. But they hadn't even dated—had they?

"I don't know what to say. I guess the cabin would be small for the two of you." Mark's mind began to race.

What exactly did Papa think he was doing? Mark was the one planning a proposal. He and Angela were going to live in the farmhouse, and Caroline too. That was if Angela said yes. And if she wasn't having second thoughts. Maybe he hadn't asked her yet, but how could Papa do this?

"Think about it. I'm heading into town to check on repairs to the old tractor. We want it workin' for the hay rides."

"How soon do you need to know? I mean, you haven't proposed yet, right?"

"No, but it's good to take care of any possible objections a girl might have, right at the start. No sense in given her extra reasons to say no."

Right, no extra reasons to say no. Which was exactly why Mark had added on to the farmhouse.

"Have you even taken Mrs. Shaw on a date? Isn't it a little early to be thinking about a proposal?"

"I hate to break it to you. Me and Mrs. Shaw—we don't have as much time as all that. Our courtship needs to grow like a white pine or, better yet, one of those hybrid poplar trees. When you're young, I guess you can act like a cedar or a spruce—take your time and ease into things. But even then you don't want to miss the plantin' season."

Brett knocked on Mark's partially open office door.

"Uh, Mark, someone here to see you," he said.

Mark paused from answering an email. "You can show them back," Mark said.

"Are you sure?" Brett opened the door wider and shifted his weight. It wasn't like Brett to hesitate. He'd worked on the farm with Papa and Mark the last six years since high school and was usually friendly toward everyone on the farm and in Sutton.

"Who is it?" Mark asked.

"John . . . Jackson."

Mark froze momentarily. "What's he doing here?" he asked. Then he stood, thanked Brett, and told him he would escort the man off the property himself.

As he walked to the front of the farmhouse, he wondered if there could be another John Jackson that had come with business for the farm. Of course there wasn't. How could the man think he could walk onto the farm and not get thrown off just as fast?

"Good to see you, Mark. Real good to see you," John said before Mark could get within handshaking distance.

Why was John acting so friendly? He certainly had a lot of nerve, showing up unannounced, uninvited.

"What are you doing here?" Mark asked, maintaining his composure. He stopped beside the sales counter.

"Thought I'd come see about a tree for the mall this year. We need a tall one, at least twenty-five feet. Do you grow any that big? Thirty would be better. What's your tallest tree? How about we start there?"

"I'm surprised you're asking, John. You mean you don't have every tree measured and tagged on some map in your office?"

"Hey, no hard feelings, right? Just because you refused the best offer you'll ever see for this place doesn't mean we can't still do business. It doesn't bother *me* at all."

"No, I don't suspect it does," Mark said with what felt like a bad taste in his mouth. "Look, I'm not interested in being buddies."

"I didn't say anything about being friends. I thought you'd like the business. The Auburn mall wants a taller tree than they had last year, and I thought of you. This is as straightforward a deal as you can get."

John and the word *straightforward* were an odd couple. Mark scanned John's posture and sideways grin and resisted the urge to throw him off the property. Maybe he was overreacting. What could be underhanded about wanting to buy one tree? After all, Mark had succeeded in keeping the land and trees out of John's hands last year. So why this fresh anger?

"How's Natalie?" Mark asked dryly.

John looked around at the chairs by the fireplace. "Don't know." He hung his head, then lifted it back up again. "We split up. Hope you're not still sore about her. She wasn't your type."

"Right. Look, if the Auburn mall is looking for one of our specialty trees, I'm happy to supply it. Why don't you give me the number of someone else, maybe the community relations rep or a facilities coordinator? Someone who hasn't tried to fraudulently purchase the farm."

John's eyes narrowed and his lips tightened. "I see. That's how you want it. Fine. I'll give your name to Roxie. She does the holiday décor. I'll stay out of it, but make sure you sell your tallest tree to us—Auburn has a reputation of prosperity to protect."

Mark held his tongue. There were a few choice words he could use to describe *John's* reputation, and *prosperous* wasn't one of them.

"It's too bad," John said as he walked to the door. He stopped with his hand on the handle. "I'm a better friend than you give me credit for. Had you taken my offer, I would have saved you the headache. You wouldn't have this mess on your hands." He made a sweeping motion with his other arm.

What was that supposed to mean? That was enough. "Go ahead and leave—and take your insults with you. Don't want to see you here again," Mark kept his voice even and calm—it helped that John was almost out the door.

Sour grapes. That's all this is.

"Not insults. Just the facts." A wicked smile broke across John's face. "You've heard, haven't you?"

Mark didn't know what he meant, but he sure didn't want to hear whatever it was from John. There wasn't much he could do about it at this point, though.

"MassDOT is working on a 'futures study' for Route 146," John said and held the next words as if he were taking aim at a target. "Looks like your farm is in the way of a planned extension. It's only a matter of time before MassDOT owns every last acre and tree here. My old buyer wouldn't be interested, but for a small finder's fee I can ask around. I guarantee I can get you more for this place than you'll get from the Commonwealth."

Mark rubbed his forehead and steadied his breathing.

John pulled an envelope out of his coat pocket, walked over, and put it on the counter near Mark. "A friend of mine works over at the transportation office. You didn't get this from me. It's a rough draft of a study that will be out sometime next year." He walked back to the door.

"Get out," Mark said.

"You could have been a wealthy man," John replied. "I don't hold grudges. I can still find you a buyer."

Mark locked eyes with John and kept his voice even. "Get out. Now."

Once John had slipped out the main door, it closed unceremoniously by itself. Mark watched to make sure he was gone, that he wasn't coming back. He grabbed the envelope off the counter and looked out the bay window. He stared at the trees long after John was out of sight. They stood resolute and didn't seem to be saying it was time for a change. Then again, had it been time to sell and he'd missed it? Wouldn't Papa have known? Surely the trees would have told him if it was time.

CHAPTER 3

It's not like Angela's mother hadn't visited unannounced before. For someone who couldn't bear the thought of driving all the way to Sutton from Providence, she'd dropped in pretty regularly this year. Every month she had a reason, a sale she'd heard about at a downtown specialty clothing store or a need to visit the farmer's market—though she had long been out of her local-foods phase. Angela attributed her visits to the fact that her mom had bought the house, but who knew? Maybe her mother would be dropping in even if she hadn't paid cash for the place and delivered it to Angela as a gift on Christmas Day.

Regardless, Angela secretly liked her mother's visits. Yes, they were inconvenient; yes, they could disrupt any plans for an afternoon, but this was better than the icy cold war they'd endured the years after Angela's marriage to Todd. And since he was long gone, it was time their grudges were too.

So here she was, rummaging through Angela's kitchen, commenting on what was in the fridge—or what wasn't.

"Honestly, I don't know how you can make a meal without a clove of garlic in the house."

Oh, the irony. Her mother hadn't cooked her own meals in years. *You mean you don't know how I can make a meal without a* chef *in the house*, Angela wanted to say but didn't. Her younger self—okay, her just-last-year-self—would have said it. But things had changed between them. Shifted. Angela couldn't pinpoint how or when it had happened. It could have been when her mother found the lost lamb from Angela's nativity and returned it to Caroline. Or the look on her mother's face when she found out that they were having Christmas dinner at the Shafer tree farm. Or maybe it was Angela's discovery that her mother had dated Mark's dad.

Whenever it had happened, she thought of her mother as more of a person now. A woman with feelings, like pain and hope. Someone with longings and sorrows instead of the one-dimensional woman—that one-dimension being constant disappointment—who'd raised Angela. Part of the shift included understanding that most of her mother's disappointment stemmed from events before Angela was even born. Like the failed engagement to Mark's dad. How could Angela have known her mother had dated him? Or that they wanted to get married—until her mom's father had intervened?

So it was easier now to smile to herself when her mother's contradictions came through so loud and clear. And it was getting easier to talk about her feelings. Sort of.

"When will you be finished managing those apartments?" Cathy asked as she surveyed the utensil drawer. "Do you have a decent paring knife?"

"Skinny drawer to the left of the stove," Angela said. "I'm only working there part-time now. Gloria from the home office has been covering two days a week, and we trade weekends. I should be done by the end of this month. Just waiting for them to hire a new manager."

"The job was supposed to be temporary. I can't believe they've held on to you this long," Cathy said.

"I've been getting paid. And believe it or not, I'll miss the tenants."

With that, her mother looked up from the apple she was cutting. "You're not serious— you *are* serious. The residents? Your life is waiting for you."

"What's that supposed to mean?" Angela asked.

"The studio, for starters. Think of the music you could be recording if you weren't over there trying to collect rent." She returned to more vigorously cutting the apple. "And your degree.

Didn't you say something about starting school this fall? You're still going to finish, aren't you? You don't have a mortgage, Caroline is at a good age, this is the perfect time to do it."

And, yes, she finished slicing the apple at the same time she wrapped up Angela's life plan, as if on cue.

"It's not that easy. I talked about starting this fall, but I wasn't sure when Blackstone would hire a new manager. And I wanted to be available to help at the tree farm."

She paused and checked her mother's face for a reaction to those words. Wanting to preempt any farm discussion, she owned up to another reason. "Besides, I still haven't decided on a major."

"Undecided," Cathy shook her head to the rhythm of the syllables.

"I know. How hard is it to figure out what I really want to do with my life?" Angela joked. "It's different now. I'm not in crisis mode. I'm not worried about making the rent payment. As crazy as it sounds, there was some simplicity to those days. I had one priority: survival. Now I have competing priorities." Angela swallowed hard before she admitted, "And I haven't figured them out yet."

"There is no figuring out to be done. You are a musician. Your major is music. End of discussion."

Any other year and that phrase *would* have ended the discussion for Angela. But she was making an effort. Instead of focusing on her mother's dyed-blonde classic bob, she chose to notice her light-blue eyes. The one thing they shared in common.

"I love my music, Mom, but there is more to the major than that. I'm not cut out for it as much as you think I am. Besides, there are other things I like."

"Such as?"

"After this year, I've learned I like business administration." She was careful not to mention that she and Mark had talked about this, about how she wanted to help run the farm.

"And what will you do with your music?" she pressed.

"If I ever want to have a music business, like producing, it would be smart to have the business background." Angela liked the sound of that as she said it. She didn't have to mention that it would be helpful at the farm, too.

"I remember a certain nineteen-year-old declaring her determination to follow her dream *and* a certain musician for as long as she lived," Cathy said emphatically, dismissing Angela's new plans.

Angela set down a stack of bowls she'd emptied from the dishwasher, pretending to steady them when it was herself she was trying to keep from wobbling. Something in her mother's tone, or perhaps the memory of her life when dreams still felt possible, took her off-center for a minute. Yes, things had shifted between her and her mother, but Cathy maintained the ability to sting—not that she did it on purpose, Angela hoped.

"I'm not nineteen now. I'll still have my music, but I don't need it to be my whole life anymore." This was an odd role reversal. Her mother defending Angela's dream and Angela sounding eerily like her mother not too many years previous.

Mom could say "I told you so" right about now.

But she didn't.

A silence ensued, and a cool September-afternoon breeze lifted the curtain away from the window.

Could it be that her mother wasn't forcing the issue to make a point? Could it be that she cared about the dream that she used to say would destroy her daughter's life? And did business administration look good to Angela because the farm looked good? Or rather, a certain tree farmer?

The door swung open, and Caroline tossed her backpack into the corner of the entry. Her golden-brown braid swung in the process. "Hi, Mom. Hi, Grandma. I didn't know you were coming today." She entered the kitchen and hugged first her mom and then her grandma before running down the hall to her bedroom.

"Mom, since you're here, could you stay for an hour or two? I was planning to take Caroline with me to the apartments while I finished up some office work, but I know she'd much rather stay here with you."

"Go with you where?" Caroline asked, rematerializing in the kitchen and scouting for a snack.

"To the apartments, but . . ." Angela looked to her mother for an answer, unsure if she wanted to be on the favor-asking side of the equation.

"Of course I can stay. I came all this way. I don't need to turn around and leave in such a hurry," she said as she smiled at Caroline.

"I'll get my book, Grandma." After a few minutes, Caroline

and Cathy were installed on the sofa reading.

That was easy. Angela grabbed her keys, but before she could get to the door her mother spoke up.

"How are you still driving that old pickup truck?"

"With my foot on the gas, Mom," Angela answered.

"Don't you think it's time for something more reliable?"

"It will be time for a new truck when there's money for a new truck."

"And why a truck?"

"I like them, that's why," she said with raised eyebrows. "And I'm going now, so thank you for staying with Caroline."

"One more thing. I've planned a little dinner this Friday for you, Caroline, and Mark. Six thirty. You can make it, right?" Cathy asked while managing to focus more on Caroline's book than on Angela.

Little dinner. Her mom never planned a little dinner.

"What for? Who else will be there?"

"Gary," she answered.

"The teacher you met this summer?" Angela asked. *Wasn't he just a nice friend?*

"He's a professor. And does there have to be a reason?" her mother asked.

"That's what you say when you're hiding something." Angela let out an exasperated sigh as she put her hand on the doorknob.

"Nothing to hide. Do you have plans? We could move it to Saturday if we make it earlier."

"No, Friday should be fine. I'll check with Mark, but I'm sure we can be there. And what reason will I give?"

"He hasn't met Gary yet. That's a good reason, isn't it?"

"Meet Gary? Does he need to? You said yourself you weren't getting serious." Angela looked to Caroline as the words left her mouth. Didn't want to go there today.

She'll have questions for me later. Who am I kidding? She'll have questions for her grandmother as soon as I walk out the door.

Angela took a step onto the porch.

"Isn't it you and Mark who are getting serious?" Cathy asked with a flash of color in her cheeks.

Caroline giggled. Angela paused to maintain her composure.

"If you're asking us to dinner to apply some kind of pressure, I'll say "No, thank you" now and save your staff the trouble."

"No, that's not it. I promise. Please come and relax."

"I'll check with Mark." Angela fumed down the porch steps to the driveway and all the way to Blackstone.

Relax? I should be worried. Very worried.

Angela settled into the manager's desk at the Blackstone apartments. Though she didn't think of it as hers anymore, she still liked the way it felt to have a place to go, a place to get some work done. Aside from Mark's farm, this little office had felt like home. But the conversation with her mother had left her second-guessing herself. Had she been wasting her time? *No.* Just the opposite. Without a mortgage payment, she'd been saving for a new truck. And wasn't it okay to like the work she'd been doing? Maybe they hadn't found someone to take her place for a reason.

The door opened with a chime of the bells that hung on the handle. Angela looked up from her maintenance requests to greet Gloria from the home office.

"Good, you're here," the woman said.

"Are those for me?" Angela asked, nodding at some files Gloria had in her hand.

"A few renewals," she said as she put them down on the desk. "There's no rush. They renew at the end of October. And, speaking of next month, we've hired a new manager."

So much for staying around here.

"Officially she'll start on the second, but I invited her to come for training. At least one week, maybe two. Did you say you'd be willing to show her some things?" Gloria asked with a cautious but pleading tone.

"Yes, I can do that," Angela answered.

Of course the end of the month and the start of the new one is the busiest time around here, but sure. Maybe another set of hands will be better than one.

"Could you go over tours? Maybe applications and contracts, too? You've handled everything so professionally. If she can follow your lead, she'll be fine," Gloria said as she sat down across the desk from Angela and checked her cell phone.

"Does she have any experience?"

"Yes, of course. Mostly sales, but she's eager to learn."

Hmm. It sounds more like she's in need of a full, two-week training, not a friendly orientation.

Maybe Angela's concern was obvious.

"Don't worry, we'll go over all the legal and accounting practices with her at the home office. Mainly we're hoping she can shadow you and learn how you do what you do so well."

"Thank you, Gloria. I'm glad to know you've been happy with what I've done. That sounds fine. Are you sure she won't mind shadowing me?"

"She seemed enthusiastic when I told her the plan," Gloria said.

Enthusiasm. That will help.

Angela didn't call to tell Mark she was coming—he would ask why and then she would end up telling him about her mother's dinner invitation over the phone, thereby defeating the purpose of talking with him face-to-face. She wanted eye contact and to see his face to make sure he was okay with it. So long as he wasn't in the middle of the farm, mowing around the trees, he wouldn't mind the surprise and they'd be able to talk.

It's just a little dinner, Angela told herself. But she knew better. She knew her mother. It would be a full-course dinner. Probably with ulterior motives for the appetizer and here's-your-life-plan for dessert.

She parked her truck in the driveway instead of the parking lot and tapped the steering wheel as she hopped out. She didn't know when it had begun, but it was a kind of thank-you to the truck for starting each time and had grown into a near-ritual—that, and asking it to start when she got back in.

She saw Mark walking toward the back lot beside the farmhouse, a clipboard in his hand. She called to him, but he didn't hear her. She picked up her pace and caught up with him as he passed the toolshed.

"Angela!" Mark reached out, hugged her with one arm, and gave her a kiss. "What are you doing here?" he asked.

She gave him a quick hug in return. "I came from the apartments. Can I join you?" she said a little breathlessly.

"I'd love your company. Doing a check on inventory for the sales lot this year."

They walked side by side as the sun moved lower in the west and a cool breeze stirred around them.

"Not sure what kind of year we'll have. Sales probably won't be as high as they were last year, but I'm counting on some of the new customers returning," Mark said.

"You mean you don't have any plans for a news story? You could call Channel Six and tell them about the "love match" trees," Angela teased. They never did find out how the station had learned about the miracle trees, though Angela suspected it was the same gentleman who'd paid for her tree that night.

"Not going to happen," Mark said. "It worked out for us, but the farm doesn't need a repeat of the chaos we had last year."

They came upon a row of trees, and Mark's paced slowed.

"Speaking of sales," Angela said, "Gloria from the home office came out to tell me they hired a new manager. She said she has sales experience."

Her excitement shifted to anxiousness. She and Mark had talked all summer about how much better it would be when her apartment-manager job ended and she could spend her time helping at the farm. But now that it was becoming a reality, she felt a pang or two of insecurity.

"Great. When does she start?"

"Not until October," Angela answered.

"Well, at least they've found someone. Do you like her?"

"I haven't met her yet. But I will soon. They asked me to show her around, do some training."

"I'm not surprised. You've had that place running better than it ever has," Mark said.

"I don't know if I would say that."

"You don't have to—it shows. Highest occupancy rate, least amount of delinquent rents. Isn't that why Gloria wanted you to stay on?"

It was a question, but only one to make his point. Angela checked Mark's face to see if there was any evidence that he thought she should keep her job there.

"Maybe. But they've found someone. So I'll be able to start work here—you know, officially—the first week of October." She sounded more hesitant than eager, all thanks to the insecurity welling up inside her.

Mark turned his attention from one of the trees, jotted something on the clipboard, and looked at Angela. "You don't have to quit, you know. If you like it there, you can stay." He said it so kindly it took Angela a minute to process what he was saying.

"So . . . you *don't* want me working at the farm?" she asked.

Mark had started walking by this time, and her question stopped him. He turned around to face her.

"Of course I do. Let me clarify. I want you to work here if *you* want to work here." He began walking again, stopping briefly at each tree and marking his clipboard.

Angela let the words sink in. He didn't elaborate, but she sensed what had been going on between the two of them.

She wanted to be at the farm with Mark, but only if he wanted her company. And Mark wanted her at the farm, so long as she really wanted to be there. And all of her checking and testing was giving him the impression that she wasn't sure she wanted to work there. That had to be the reason he'd suggested she keep her manager job. Right?

Right.

Perhaps a change of subject was in order.

"What kind of notes are you making about the trees?" she asked.

"I'm counting."

"*All* the trees? I thought maybe you estimated . . ." She looked over the tops of the trees and was staggered by the thought of having to count them one by one.

"Not all of them. Just the ones that will be ready to sell this season. We should have enough to meet demand, but we like to identify the trees that are in that sweet spot for height and shape."

Angela nodded and followed Mark's line of sight to each tree, hoping to see what he saw. She loved it here, loved being with him.

"I do want to work here, you know," Angela said quietly.

Mark had stepped in between two trees—though she thought he was close enough to still hear her.

"I was afraid of that," he said, sighing heavily.

"Excuse me?" Before he could explain, panic took over. "I knew it. I knew you didn't want me here. All this time I felt like something was off. Like you didn't want me here." She was speaking more to herself. "Is it because I grew up in the city? Is it the accident with the pruning shears this past summer?" Angela threw up her hands in exasperation.

"What are you talking about?" Mark stared at Angela. "I never said any of that."

"I just said I wanted to work here, and you said you were afraid of that.'" She forced back the tears threatening to derail the entire conversation.

"What? No! That's not what I was talking about. Brown spot—on the trees. Look here." He motioned to the back of the tree he'd been looking at, and sure enough, some of the needles were yellow and mottled. He inspected the surrounding trees. "I only see these two trees. Maybe this one here should go too. Brett and I will come out tomorrow. We'll remove these and get some fungicidal spray on the rest of this section."

Angela nodded, embarrassed yet relieved. Not that the trees had brown spot but that Mark was afraid of *it* and not *her*.

Mark made some detailed notes and began walking back toward the farmhouse. At once, Angela noticed the sun had sunk below the tree line, and though they had enough light to see their way back, it was a fading and shadow-filled light.

Once they were at the side door to the farmhouse, Angela spoke up. "Sorry about that back there. I didn't know you were talking about the trees."

Mark smiled mischievously. "You knew I didn't want you here? The pruning accident?" He opened the door and tossed his clipboard onto the counter, then turned and in one swooping motion scooped Angela up and carried her through the side door into the front room.

Am I that petite, or is he that strong?

Amid her half protest, half enjoyment, Mark spun her around in front of the fireplace and then set her down in the wingback chair. Placing his hands on each of the armrests, he bent down and kissed the side of her cheek, then the side of her lips.

"I love you, Angela. I will love you no matter where you live or where you work. But make no mistake, I want you as close to me as possible," he said as he dropped to one knee in front of the chair, gently took her face in his hands, and looked into her eyes before he kissed her more deeply.

Angela melted into Mark's soft kisses. She could hear her own breathing. And then heavy footsteps. Papa came in through the front door.

"Oh, good. You're here. Found some—"

"Scotches with Brown spot? Probably best if I have Brett remove them," Mark finished.

Papa stopped in his tracks and scratched the back of his head. "Glad you're on it!" he said and continued to the kitchen.

Mark stood, and Angela followed him. "It's late. I need to get home. My mother is there with Caroline."

She remembered the dinner plans—the reason she came to see him in the first place. "Before I go, Cathy invited us to her house this Friday for dinner."

"What did you tell her?" Mark asked matter-of-factly.

"I said I'd check with you. It's at six thirty."

"Great, I'll pick you up about five thirty," Mark said.

"Are you sure? If you're busy I can tell her we have other plans," Angela said.

"Are *you* sure? This is what, the third time she's asked us. You've said no every other time. Should I be worried there's something at her house you don't want me to see? Like do you have a shrine to Todd in your bedroom or something?"

"Wait, what? No, it's not the house." *Okay sort of, but not for the reasons you think.* "You know my mom, talking with her can be a—um, a minefield."

"You don't think I can handle a little dinner with your mom?"

"No dinner with my mom is little. And don't forget her "non-boyfriend" Gary. And, no, I'm not saying you can't handle it, just—why would you want to?"

"It's me you're talking to. Cathy and I get along fine. At some point she may not feel the need to tell me about my dad and how long they dated every time she sees me. She's your mother, and I love you. Trust me, there isn't anything that could change the way I feel about you."

Right. How about a butler and a full-course meal?

Angela watched Mark as he said the words. His eyes were focused on her with a genuine expression. "I hope you mean that," she said, but she still had the nagging worry that her mother might try to force the engagement issue. So what if it had been eight months or nine? Who was counting? No need to rush. They would do this on their time, not Cathy's.

Mark walked Angela to the door.

Papa returned from the kitchen eating the last of his sandwich. He waved and offered his four words, "Good to see ya."

Angela paused before leaving. "So I'll tell her we can make it?" The question in her voice drew a chuckle from Mark.

"Yes. We'll be there."

"You know my mom, she is probably going to bring up *us*."

"And? Is that a bad thing?" Mark asked.

"No, but I don't want it to be awkward if she asks."

"Asks what?"

"About us getting engaged." There, she'd named the elephant.

"So I should bring the ring? Wear my suit?"

Angela could hear the teasing in his voice. He was baiting her, and she knew it.

"Yes, bring the ring. A proposal at *her* dinner table—my nightmare and my mother's dream."

"I may just do that."

"You wouldn't."

"I could," Mark said.

"But you wouldn't," Angela insisted.

"We'll see."

CHAPTER 4

Mark read the papers John Jackson had left—what he'd claimed would bring the end of the Shafer tree farm. There were about sixteen pages of a "possible" futures study. For a rough draft, it contained some specific details—goals, processes, recommendations. There in black-and-white print with aerial color photos was the planned expansion of Route 146 including the need for a frontage road right through the southern section of the property. Proof that the farm was at risk.

What the pages didn't include was a 1-800 number to call with questions, complaints, or rebuttals. Only the names of the governor and secretary of transportation. And an address for the Executive Office of Transportation Planning. And reasons. Lots of reasons for their proposal, like a reduction in traffic congestion and an improvement in safety—all things for the good of the people of the Commonwealth.

There wasn't much said about the farm. A few lines was all it took to put it on the map of properties to be acquired for "the purposes of MassDOT to construct a frontage road and provide ample space for revised interchange geometry," thereby facilitating a "wider roadway to ease congestion."

Ease congestion. Remove trees to make room for more cars.

Mark tossed the papers onto his bed. Lousy study. Lousy John Jackson. He picked up his guitar and walked through the empty house to clear his mind. He arrived at the new rooms he'd added on, pulled back the hanging plastic, and walked over the new wooden floors. He strummed the chords to Angela's song. He'd written it just for her. Once he had one more piece of equipment, he could record her song. And one night soon, he could propose.

He walked to the full-length window. The rising moon cast a silver light across the trees. He let his mind drift for a few moments, imagining their life together, hoping Angela would love it here as much as he did. Other girls he'd dated—okay, *every* girl he had dated—thought the trees were quaint, but they weren't interested in making them their life's work. And Natalie, she had taken it one step further and nearly convinced Mark to sell everything and try to make a living with his music. Of course, had she truly loved him and not been dating John Jackson at the same time—he might have gone through with the deal and made the biggest mistake of his life.

But he hadn't. And that was when Angela had come into his life. She and her daughter fit right in at the farm. And he wanted them to feel at home. He wanted this to be their home.

The light was out in Papa's cabin. It was a little early for him to be turning in. Mark set his guitar down and walked over to the side door and grabbed his coat. It couldn't hurt to check on him.

When he opened the door, Papa was there on his front step. A gust of wind came in the house before he did.

"Goin' somewhere?" Papa asked.

"Yeah, to check on you."

"What for? I'm right here."

Mark chuckled to himself. "I can see that now."

"Have you thought about my offer?"

"What offer is that?" Mark asked.

"Trading places?" Papa said as he walked across the front room past the cash register and down the hall.

"If you're sure about Mrs. Shaw and you think it will help the cause." Mark's voice trailed off. He'd followed Papa to where he now stood in the doorway of the newly added rooms.

"I can move my things over tonight. How about you?" Papa asked, not looking at Mark but scanning the sound equipment in the room.

"Tonight? I hadn't thought so soon. I'm working on a few things here."

"I can see that. Looks like an airplane cockpit."

Mark sighed. *So much for surprises.* "It's a recording studio," he explained.

Papa turned and walked over to the spacious area. "Then what's this, another dining room?" he asked.

"Actually, a dance floor," Mark said sheepishly.

Papa's face registered surprise, accompanied by a smile. "Wouldn't have thought our tree farm needed one, but something tells me this isn't just for you."

"I want to surprise Angela, remember?"

"Have you proposed yet?"

Mark shook his head.

"Sure going to a heap a' trouble for a girl you aren't even sure is planning to stay with you." Papa's face had a grave expression, but his mouth turned up into a smirk. "Looks like you're bettin' she'll say yes, too."

Mark walked over to the studio and turned on the sound system. He played a recording of one of his older songs, and the music came through loud and clear, filling the whole room. Mark came back to Papa's side.

"That's just it. Remember what you were saying about Mrs. Shaw and taking care of any objections she might have? If I'm asking Angela to marry me and to live here, I thought it only right that she have a place to work on her music."

Papa didn't speak but nodded.

"I want her to love it here as much as I do," Mark insisted.

"And the dance floor, does her house have one of those too?" Papa asked.

"No. That was my idea. Something new for both of us."

"At least you've been thinking 'bout someone else's happiness besides your own," Papa declared. "Do you have any more of that plastic?"

"Yes, why?"

"Let's put it up. As far as anyone else is concerned, this will be under construction while me and Mrs. Shaw are here. If this is something for you and Angela, we need to keep it that way," Papa said as he walked out of the room. "I'm going to get my things. How long will it take you to pack?"

A short time later, Mark had tossed some clothes, an alarm clock, and his toothbrush into a duffel bag. He gathered some of his pictures and sheet music and set them in a small bin. Papa returned quickly. Mark pulled his boots from his closet and rummaged for the box they came in.

"Set your bags over by the dresser," he called to Papa. "I don't have much more to pack."

"I only have one," Papa said. "By my age, you learn that if it doesn't fit in one bag, you probably don't need it."

Mark grabbed his backpack and tossed it into the hallway.

"What's this?" Papa asked, holding up some papers that had been on Mark's bed.

Not those.

"That's some research I was—" Mark held his hand out, but it was too late. Papa sat down on the bed and began to read.

"Department of Transportation research?" Papa mumbled.

"Look, it's not important, and it's getting late. I know you like to turn in early."

Papa waved Mark's hand away.

Mark sighed and sat down on the bed. As long as Papa lost interest and didn't turn the page. As long as he didn't see where Shafer Farm was listed as a—

"Potential property to be acquired for the expansion of Route 146," Papa read out loud.

Mark put his head into his hands for a minute. He wanted to tell Papa once he had it figured out.

"What's not important about this? Looks to me like it might be more important than everything else we've been talking about." Papa handed him the papers. "Were you going to tell me, son?"

Mark knew the gravity of the situation when his grandfather called him that.

"Yes, but I didn't want to worry you. At least not yet. John Jackson brought those papers when he came asking for the tallest tree we had. I wasn't even sure he was telling the truth."

"Looks like he was."

"Here's the thing. It's just a study. They haven't even published it."

"Yet," Papa said.

"If there's a way to stop the acquisition process before it begins, we're fine."

"And if there isn't?" Papa asked with a furrowed brow.

Mark stood and paced the room. "I don't know. I hope it doesn't come to that." Mark looked at Papa and tried to make eye contact, but his grandfather's eyes were fixed on the floor. "Papa, should I have sold this farm last year? While we had a buyer, you know, instead of losing it to the state?"

Papa stood and slapped his leg. "'Course not!" he scoffed. "We're tree keepers."

"Right," Mark said, starting to feel reassured.

"Nothin' is going to get in the way of that," Papa continued.

"Exactly," Mark said again, reinforcing his feeling of resolve.

"Unless the Commonwealth bulldozes these trees. Then we're done for," Papa concluded, sitting back down on the bed and loosening the laces on his boots.

"Wait, what?"

"Not gonna worry about it tonight. Now, have you got all you need so I can get a decent night's sleep?"

Mark gathered up his things. "Yes, I'm going, but shouldn't we do something? Walk the lot tomorrow and talk about a strategy?"

"Or you could call your lawyer friend downtown," Papa said.

"You mean my real estate agent's brother Jeff?" Mark asked, realizing that made the most sense.

"Unless you've got another friend in the legal business."

"Great idea. I'll look him up," Mark said as he headed for the door.

"Wait a minute. Here's an extra blanket. Nights are startin' to get chilly in the cabin." Papa pulled the comforter off the bed.

"Thanks, but what about you—here?"

"I'll be just fine. Probably too hot with all the insulation."

"One more thing." Mark stood with his backpack on his shoulder, his duffel bag in his hand, and his other hand clutching the bulk of the comforter. "How long do you plan on staying in the farmhouse?"

"At the rate you're moving, I'd say Mrs. Shaw and I have plenty of time."

There was a pause, and Mark looked away from Papa.

Papa must have picked up on the meaning behind Mark's question. "We won't stay one day longer than we need to. This place is yours when you need it."

"Where will you and Mrs. Shaw go?"

"Things have a way of working out." Papa stretched out his arms and clasped them behind his head. "If the trees haven't taught you that yet, they will soon."

Papa hadn't been kidding about the cabin. Forty-nine degrees wasn't cold by winter standards, but with the humidity it felt colder. Mark unpacked his duffel bag and moved his clothes to the old pine dresser—furniture his great-grandfather had made. More solid and with a few decorative touches that were hard to find in the manufactured furniture they sold downtown. He pulled out a long-sleeved T-shirt and a pullover. A few degrees colder and he'd be able to see his breath.

Tomorrow he'd bring his guitar and some of his music to the cabin. And maybe look into a space heater. There were a few lines of Angela's song he wanted to work on. He reached for the backpack and pulled out his alarm clock. He searched the room for the one outlet, which meant the clock would need to sit on the floor on the other side of the room.

The song was mostly done. So was the studio. The only other thing he needed was the ring—he wanted to give her the one they'd found in the box last Christmas, the one he'd slipped onto Angela's finger—which she had promptly given back, of course. They hadn't even started dating yet. It had been a spontaneous gesture, and he smiled at the memory. And at the kiss they'd shared. Unexpected, but from what he remembered, enjoyable.

A new worry crept in.

Maybe she wouldn't like that ring.

Would she want a new one? After all, he wasn't quite sure where the ring had come from. Maybe his grandmother or his great-grandmother. He didn't know.

He reclined on the bed, his head hitting the headboard a little too hard as he did so. He grabbed the pillow, punched it, and then put it back under his head. Was he as ready as he thought he was? All this time preparing and he might need a new ring. Or, at the very least, get to the bottom of who owned the ring from the box.

Finish the song. Finish the studio. Visit the jewelry store.

And while I'm at it, save the farm from becoming a frontage road.

After finding the number for Owens and Dunne Law, Mark called and spoke to Jeff Dunne. Most of what he remembered about Jeff was his record-setting basketball games in high school. He hoped he was as successful in his law career.

"Supposing the inside information you have turns out to be accurate, until you receive notification as the property owner, there isn't much you can do."

That was exactly opposite of what Mark wanted to hear.

"Doesn't knowing all of this now help us?"

"If you want to check some other MassDOT projects—look for businesses, homeowners, anyone who had fought them before and won. Then I can check some of the Department of Transportation reports for you. But that's about it until you get an official notice."

Not as much help as Mark was hoping for.

The memory of John Jackson's grin and exaggerated words about "the best offer you'll ever have" returned to him. Of course, he'd dismissed it when he'd said it. There wasn't even a question in Mark's mind that he'd done the right thing.

But now the prospect of losing the land to the state raised a new question. Was it too late to sell to someone other than John Jackson? If the planned extension was as inevitable as it seemed, should he find a buyer before it became common knowledge?

He looked up from the report he was reading and glanced over his shoulder. He was alone. And he wasn't doing anything wrong, but the mere thought of selling the farm prompted a rush of guilt.

Could he find another buyer? There were some who looked for land that had been marked as possible eminent domain—those willing to take a gamble that the government might do more studies and not end up acquiring the property.

Mark stood and walked to the window. Here he could see the trees and the north wind blowing furiously through them. A calmness, as gentle as the wind was angry, crept over him. He could see some of the new seedlings holding their own against the coming storm. *We will stay.*

It was Mark's thought, crisp and clear, but it had come to the forefront of his mind unaided. And that settled it. Of course they would stay. And Mark would fight whatever plans MassDOT would make. Sutton didn't need a new road over these acres. It needed these trees. He didn't know how, but he would protect the land and trees.

Mark returned to the Internet, searching through the settlements. He found case after case of people and companies who had settled with the good Commonwealth of Massachusetts. Not what he was looking for.

He noticed an article on a revised MassDOT project. Revised due to an inability to secure the proposed land. Why? He read through to the end of the page, letting it soak in.

The land was home to a 150-year-old church, and that church was conveniently listed on the National Register of Historic Places.

Not that his farm and that church had anything in common, but this was at least one example of the Department of Transportation not getting their way. Maybe the cabin or the land had some historical significance. He could ask Papa. It was possible, wasn't it?

Get the farm listed on the National Register.

How hard could it be?

CHAPTER 5

Mark, Angela, and Caroline waited outside her mother's door. Her grand and imposing front door.

"Can't we just knock and walk in tonight?" Caroline asked. "She knows we're coming."

Angela glanced at Mark and then explained, "Grandma Elliott is a bit more formal than that. Besides, you wouldn't want to hurt Walters's feelings, would you?"

The door opened wide, and Walters greeted Angela warmly, took her jacket, and gave Mark one of his signature once-over looks. They stepped into the entryway onto imported tile. Caroline bounded through the door between them, hugging Walters around one of his legs. He patted her on the head, though stiffly. His silver hair had thinned considerably since the last time Angela had visited, though his motions were no slower and he maintained his characteristic straight-backed posture.

"Mark, this is Walters," Caroline said.

Angela turned and whispered loud enough for Walters to hear, "He's not as tough as he looks. Unless you are a teenage girl trying to escape out your bedroom window. Then watch out."

"Got it," Mark said with a smile. "No window exits."

Walters nodded, and once Caroline had released him, he

escorted them under a massive chandelier and past the study with the American antique collection.

"This house was like my mother's other child," Angela explained, unaffected.

"You're calling this place a house?" Mark replied.

Angela continued. "If I needed winter clothes, the house needed winter draperies. If I needed swim lessons, the house needed a new pool house."

On they went until greeted by Angela's mother, who was dressed in a royal-blue sweater, black skirt, and far too many diamonds—earrings, necklace, and bracelets. She glinted and glimmered her way over to them at the entrance to the dining room. "Please, come sit down. Gary will be back in a moment. He went to check on Bones."

They paused. Had Angela missed something? Caroline, never fearful of the obvious, asked, "Who's Bones, Grandma?"

At that, a dark, curly-haired dog trotted into the room, followed by a tall, slender, well-dressed man. She brushed by Cathy's leg and approached Caroline, stopped, sat on her hind feet, and put a paw up.

"*This* is Bones, Gary's dog."

Angela could see Caroline was already smitten. It was love at first paw shake. Though that was easily understandable. Caroline had asked for a dog every so often, but Angela had put her off. They couldn't afford one. The apartments didn't allow them. There was always a reason.

Gary was losing his non-boyfriend status over this as far as Angela was concerned. Knowing her mother's aversion to shedding hair and the potential lack of bladder control, how she could allow a *friend* to bring his dog with him served to reinforce one thing in Angela's mind. He had to be more than a friend.

"I know what you're thinking, Angela," Cathy said. "And the answer is yes, Caroline is welcome to spend time here when Gary and Bones are here."

She needs to work on her mind reading.

"Actually, I was wondering what kind of dog he is."

And how much you must like Gary to let him bring one through the door.

"A Portuguese water dog, right, Gary?" Cathy said.

He nodded. Caroline petted and cooed.

"Bones brings so much life to this house—this oversized museum of a house. I don't know why I didn't think having a pet here sooner."

Mark raised his eyebrows at Angela when her mother used the word *museum*—he'd want brownie points for that.

She needed to get to know this Gary if he could work this kind of magic with her mother. Turn-her-worldview-upside-down kind of magic.

"Mark, this is Dr. Gary Wilson, professor of anthropology at the University of Rhode Island. Gary, this is Mark Shafer—owner of the Shafer Tree Farm in Sutton," Cathy said. Angela noted her mother's stress on the word *owner*.

Gary casually shook Mark's hand, then Angela's.

"Nice to meet you Dr. Wilson," Mark said.

"Please, call me Gary," he said as he knelt down beside Caroline and Bones. "He likes you, I can see. After dinner I'll show you his house."

The dog has a house here?

Gary took Bones out while they were seated at the table. Something about the dog's wagging tail helped Angela relax. Maybe her mother had mellowed, maybe this dinner would not be the grilling she expected.

"So when *are* you two going to get serious about the future?" Cathy asked before drinks.

Maybe not.

Angela looked away from her mother, mostly in disbelief, partly to take a sharp, deep breath before answering. She caught Mark's mischievous grin out of the corner of her eye. Her palms began to sweat, she reached for the fancy-folded napkin on the table and unfurled it on her lap.

He wouldn't. Would he?

"Funny you should ask, Cathy," Mark said, looking to her, then to Angela, then to Caroline.

Angela couldn't tell if he was teasing or preparing. She paused long enough to make sure he wasn't reaching for a ring, and then she spoke up. "What do you mean by serious? Mark's coming over tomorrow to help me record another song for my album."

Caroline played with the dessert spoon set at the top of her plate, tracing the embroidered pattern on the tablecloth. "I think she means your *marriage* future, not your *music* future."

Mark laughed at that. Angela frowned.

Gary returned to the room. "What did I miss?"

"Some wedding-pressure hors d'oeuvres," Mark answered.

"Oh?" he looked to Cathy. "And how do those taste?" he asked with a smirk. What was it between them? Angela wasn't sure.

"I don't know what you're talking about," Cathy declared. She began describing the meal to come in such great detail that no one approached the other subject again.

Not until later did Angela think about the timing of her mother's question, conveniently when Gary was out of the room.

Finally, dessert was cleared, and the conversation slowed. Angela noticed the pattern Caroline had been tracing on the tablecloth. Bright yellows and reds, intricate florals. She admired it for a moment before the recognition set in.

"Dona Florinda," Angela said out loud.

"Excuse me?" Cathy said.

"This tablecloth and these napkins—Florinda gave them to us, right?" She remembered now. Florinda had done the needlework herself—something she did when she missed her mother and Portugal.

"Yes, that's right," Cathy said. "I thought you might appreciate them."

Angela ran her hand over the stitches, happy for the memory but suddenly feeling a bit melancholy. She had loved her piano lessons and former teacher, but it was more than that. Florinda held a place in her heart. She was someone who had taught her about herself and the world, and in such a caring way. How could she not?

Oh, Florinda—I wish you could meet Mark.

She must have been staring too long or allowing that longing to show on her face.

"For goodness' sake, Angela. If you like them that much you can have them."

Angela heard the disappointment in her mother's voice. Obviously she wanted Angela to appreciate the linens, not pine for them.

Angela shook off the thought. "No, Mom, keep them here. She made them specifically for this table." Though Angela had no idea if that were true, it seemed the most believable reason for her not to take them and further wound her mother's feelings.

"I know she was dear to you. When was the last time you heard from her?" Cathy asked.

"Christmas, the year after Caroline was born. She sent a card," Angela answered. "But that was before she left the States, I think." Again, Angela didn't know. That had been a difficult time, and she'd hadn't done a good job of staying in touch.

Caroline asked to see Bones. Cathy cleared her throat. "Before you go see him, there is a matter, a rather important matter, I wanted to discuss."

Angela heard the formality in her voice. Was she trying to bring up their engagement again? Or was there something even more awkward on her agenda?

Caroline appeared unmoved and looked to Gary for hope at leaving the table.

He smiled back at Caroline and then spoke. "Cathy has wanted to tell you for some time that she is going to Europe. In two weeks."

Angela looked to her mother's face for confirmation of this. She found in her mother's eyes an uncharacteristically soft expression, a pleading expression. But why?

"Europe?" Angela asked. Of course, it was a one-word question, as if to confirm she heard the location correctly. But it included everything else—*in two weeks? Alone? Is Gary going? How long have you been planning this? Why take so long to tell me?*

"That's great news," Mark said easily.

"Are you taking Bones?" Caroline asked while Angela was still stunned.

"No, Gary isn't coming. I'm going alone. Well, mostly."

"What does that mean?" Angela asked.

"Remember the Fiddlemans? We've had this trip planned for years."

"Dad's college roommate? And his wife . . . What was her name? Nancy. They've been inviting you to visit them since they relocated . . . over fifteen years ago. Didn't you and Dad plan a trip?" Angela checked herself, remembering Gary was at the table. "Their invitation is still open?" she asked. Though she wished she didn't sound—or feel—so protective.

"Yes, that's right. Your father and I made plans. He knew I'd dreamt of going. We'd tell the Fiddlemans we were coming, then something would come up. The campaign finance fiasco. Or the governor's assignment on a special task force for something. I don't know. The war on drugs. But there was always something until it wasn't an option. Until now." She smiled gently at Gary, throwing Angela even more.

"So Bones is not going to Europe?" Caroline asked.

"Bones and I are staying here," Gary told her softly.

Caroline sat against the back of her chair and smiled, a bit pleased with herself.

"For how long?" Angela asked. She knew her mother wouldn't go unless she could spend more than two weeks. Every year she didn't make the trip, there was more she wanted to see when she did make the trip. Father would joke that if they waited long enough, she'd have so much to see they'd need dual citizenship and may not make it back.

"At least a month," Gary announced with a slight edge to his voice. Angela wondered what that meant.

"Do I have to wait that long before I can see him again?" Caroline asked, referring to the dog. Angela hoped her mother would not take it personal that Caroline seemed much more concerned about missing a dog she'd just met than her grandmother.

"We could work out an arrangement," Gary offered.

"Don't the Fiddlemans already live in France?

"They do," Cathy answered, unmoved.

"So you're traveling alone? By yourself?" Angela knew they'd been discussing the dog. But this point was more disconcerting to her than potential pet-visiting hours.

"Yes I am," Cathy said emphatically. She held her coffee cup a bit too rigidly, though, and looked to Gary with pleading eyes again.

Gary paused and then offered some explanation. "She's been trying to talk me into retiring."

This was interesting. Cathy was quite used to getting her way. And as much as Gary appeared to care for her mother, Angela could see he had no intention of ending his professorship early for a Europe tour. She watched Cathy carefully.

"I thought you could apply for one of those sabbaticals, or whatever they're called."

"The university would ask for a report. I'd need research or a few speaking engagements. That's not how you want to tour

Europe." He answered calmly but left Angela with the impression he and her mother had discussed this before.

"She could wait two more years for me," he said with a glance toward Cathy.

"You know this is the year I—it has to be this year. The Fiddlemans are moving back to the States." Cathy's face flushed a bit, her eyes resting on a spot of carpet.

Now this was adding up. Cathy didn't want to miss the chance to see her friends, the safety of their accommodations, and company.

"Good grief, if that's all this is about—wanting to see Europe with Nancy—then go. You don't have to act as if you only have six months to live," Angela said, relieved to finally understand the reason for her mother's insistence.

Cathy moved in her chair and looked distractedly about the room and back and forth to Mark and Angela.

"What is it, Mom? Is there something else?"

"You'll think I'm being pushy or controlling. But I want to know your plans before I head off. I don't want to miss . . . I want to make sure I'm around for any *big event* in your life." She said it so meekly Angela didn't recognize her own mother.

Things clicked into place. She did have a reason for the dinner. And for asking about their possible engagement. Angela even sensed worry in her voice. She was leaving the country and didn't want to miss out. This realization brought a wave of relief with it, though Angela didn't know why, as her mother still waited expectantly for the answer to the same question she'd asked at the beginning of dinner.

"Don't worry. If you're only going for a month, nothing can happen that fast around here," Angela said with a nervous laugh.

Mark reached over, took her hand, and looked at her with his genuine eyes, his irresistible eyes.

"I don't mind if you get engaged while I'm gone, but I would hope you would wait for my return before any kind of ceremony," Cathy said, directing her words to Mark.

Only Mark couldn't have known why her mother felt the need to *ask* to be invited to their wedding. And why she was asking so timidly. This had everything to do with Angela's first marriage to Todd and her mother's refusal to attend the wedding. If she dwelt on it, the pain would return, and with it the desire to exclude her mother. But that was over nine years ago. They were speaking again and getting along now. Of course they would invite her.

But how had the conversation come to this? They weren't engaged, and even if Mark asked Angela tonight, they wouldn't have a wedding in a month! Had Angela missed something?

"Angela, could I . . . could we talk . . . maybe in the other room?" Mark asked.

He took her by the hand, and led her out of the room. Angela wasn't sure why or what was happening. She could hear Caroline asking more Bones questions. They walked to the parlor and sat on one of Cathy's custom-upholstered sofas, and Mark began talking in quiet tones about Cathy's expressions and a mother's love for her daughter, and how important engagements could be. Angela was only half listening, distracted by her own mental replay of everything that had been said at the table.

"Wait, what did you say about engagements?" Angela asked.

"That maybe it would put your mother at ease if we were engaged before she left," Mark said plainly.

"You're not joking, are you?"

"No, Angela. You saw your mother's face. She isn't trying to manipulate us. This means a lot to her."

It was true. Even if it was a departure for her mother. But Angela felt that familiar off-the-rails feeling anyway. She noticed Mark's posture, and a flash of panic filled her chest.

"No," she said. "Don't do this Mark."

"Do what?" he asked.

"Don't you dare propose here—not in my mother's house, not on this sofa," Angela's voice rose. "I know something is different, but don't you see? She'll get her way. It will be on her terms."

"Angela, I only meant to say we could give her some encouragement," Mark said.

"If you propose to me now, it will feel like my mom is running my life again."

Mark leaned over and kissed her. On the cheek, on the lips. It surprised her but calmed her at the same time.

"No one is running your life but you."

She took a much-needed deep breath in between his kisses.

He continued. "I want to marry you. That doesn't surprise you, does it? But I'm not asking tonight, not until it's the right time for both of us. And I won't ask at all if you don't want to marry me." He looked into her eyes, holding her gaze. "Do you want to marry me? Not *will* you, but do you *want* to?" He whispered the questions, but didn't wait for answers. He kissed her again, and she melted into him.

Yes. Yes! She *wanted* to marry him. But fresh memories of her marriage to Todd—and the painful end of it were sounding alarm bells in her head now. What would it take for her to be sure she wasn't making another mistake?

Though Mark's kisses could cause her to forget where she was and who she was, the designer upholstery reminded her of everyone waiting in the other room. This wasn't the best time for her to get lost in one of Mark's irresistible embraces.

"Yes," she whispered back. "You always know the right thing to say."

They returned to their chairs, Angela a bit breathless, Mark pleasantly calm.

"Cathy, I don't think your long-awaited tour of Europe is in danger of being cut short by any sudden matrimony."

All eyes were on Angela, even though Mark had spoken.

"But you know how it is over at the Shafer Tree Farm. Anything can happen." He winked at Caroline. "Make sure we have a way to contact you."

The cushioned wicker love seat on the screened porch at Angela's house was a welcome change for Mark and Angela's post-dinner conversation. Caroline had protested somewhat before settling into bed but had finally fallen asleep.

Angela dished up two small bowls of chocolate ice cream.

"Lights? No lights?" she asked.

He said, "Whatever you like," so she left them off. The streetlamp from two houses away filtered in through the screens, causing the furniture and wooden floor to glow. Their faces were visible but in a soft, obscured way. This Angela loved. The sheer comfort of sitting close in the semidarkness on a porch that should theoretically feel exposed, but at night it was like they became part of the fixtures—hidden in plain sight.

Their conversation slowed to a stop-and-go, thoughtful pace. Long pauses felt natural, their questions floating in the air a minute or two before one of them would answer. Subjects changed effortlessly from one thing to another. This connectedness, Angela loved too.

"It's late," Mark said. "Do you have an early morning?"

"Not as early as you. And you still have a drive," Angela replied. "Did I scoop too much?" she asked, motioning to the bowl of ice cream.

"Not at all. This hits the spot."

There was a comfortable silence while they both ate. Angela thought about the driving Mark had done over the summer, the miles through town, back and forth. For her. And unlike Cathy, he'd never complained. Not once. For all her panicking at Cathy's house, she now had a twinge of sympathy in her chest. *Mark has been so patient.*

"You know, we could do something about that," Angela said before she thought too much about it.

"About what?" Mark was clearly too lost in his ice cream to follow her train of thought.

"About the driving. We could shorten the distance," she said, surprising herself. But their conversation at her mother's house was having an effect on her.

Mark eyed her carefully. She waited for what she was suggesting to sink in.

"Did I miss a season?" Mark said. "Aren't we waiting four seasons so you can be sure about me?" he asked with a good-natured laugh. "So what do you think of Gary?" he asked, changing the subject.

I'm probably confusing him, Angela thought. *I'm confusing myself!*

"I don't know what to think. Before tonight I would have told you he was rather unassuming. When she met him in the summer, I thought for sure it would be over once the school year began. Then I find out my mom has a house for his *dog*."

"So you think there's more going on there?" Mark asked, moving his arm around Angela after putting down the bowl.

She felt his hand rest easily on her shoulder. Such a small touch and yet it distracted her every time.

"He isn't going with her to Europe. So there is that," Angela said. "We'll see what happens after her trip. I wonder if she'll feel the same about him after Barcelona and Milan."

"What? No Paris or Madrid?"

"I'm sure she'll stop there, too. And probably London and who knows where else. Cathy has eclectic interests. Every year she planned to go, she had her reasons. Now they've all morphed into one giant adventure. She took an architecture class. Barcelona's got the gothic thing going on. Of course, exotic food has been a constant. And shopping. I'm not sure how she's going to bring all the Versace and Prada home."

Angela smiled at the thought of her mother trying to fit it all in, buying more designer luggage in the process. She rested her head against Mark's chest and closed her eyes.

"Will you be okay if Gary turns out to be more than a non-boyfriend for your mom?" Mark asked it in such a serious, knowing way, like he knew something she didn't.

"Of course. I don't mind Gary. If I think about it, he's good for my mom. She needs the company."

"That's just it. Ever since you and your mom reconciled last Christmas, you've been able to spend more time together. More this year than the last five put together, you said not that long ago. Are you sure you wouldn't feel, I don't know, like it was too soon to let her go again?"

He was right. So right. That *was* how she'd been feeling without being able to put words to it. And yet it didn't make any sense. Gary wasn't possessive, and Cathy had been, on the whole, much happier.

"Yeah, that is what it feels like," Angela reluctantly admitted. "But how did you know that?"

"Why do you think I haven't proposed yet?"

The question blindsided her. What did Gary and Cathy have to do with Mark's proposal? Angela sat up to look at him, squinting in the half-light.

"Because like some superstitious fool I told you we needed to know each other four seasons. Or maybe you don't like the way I prune the trees."

Angela knew it wasn't her tree-pruning debacle, but she did wonder if he'd had second thoughts and if the four seasons had worked against them somehow.

Mark laughed a head-shaking laugh. "Right, you've mentioned the four seasons rule a time or two before," he said.

Angela waited. There was more, and her mind couldn't quite grasp it. "Are you going to tell me, or do I need to keep guessing?"

"You and your mom, you've been getting along and spending time together, and Caroline has loved it. I didn't want to ask too soon, move too quickly, and take you from this time with her."

Patient, insightful. And selfless. And what have I been? Obsessed with four seasons and not making another mistake.

CHAPTER 6

As Mark drove to Angela's house across town, he reviewed their conversation from the night before. No, there was one sentence in particular he replayed over and over.

"We could shorten the distance," she'd said. Her expression had been playful, her eyes flirtatious, even. That one comment had sparked so much hope in him he wanted to ask her to marry him right on the spot. But given how she'd been acting at her mother's house, he'd chosen to focus on his ice cream instead. He planned to ask soon, though. And then they could shorten the distance.

When he arrived at Angela's house, she was finishing the dishes. She dried her hands and came and gave him a hug. She rested her head on his shoulder. Her thick, curly hair had been partially pulled back. He closed his eyes for a minute. This was an ordinary moment, but Angela lingered a little longer than usual, and it felt like this was their house and that they belonged together. And he liked the way that felt. He liked the way *she* felt.

"I brought a little something for Caroline." Mark set his bag down and took it out.

Angela tipped her head. "A picture of a pine tree?"

"Not any tree—the one she picked out for Christmas. She's been asking if she could go visit it, so I thought, why not bring the tree to her? Where is she?"

She brushed the back of his arm with her hand. "Not here. She's actually with my mom," she said. "That was sweet of you."

"In Providence?" Mark asked.

"The very place. She begged to play with Bones before Cathy leaves."

Mark thought for a minute. "It's not Cathy's dog, right?"

"My mom said Gary would be visiting. Believe me, I'm all for Caroline playing with Bones at her house."

"Are we picking her up tonight? How much time do we have?" Mark asked. He pulled the sheet music from his bag. Angela eyed it and smiled.

"As much as we need. You know, you hinted on the phone that tonight might be special?" Angela moved into the kitchen and pulled out drinks.

"I did?" Mark's mind raced over their phone call earlier that day. They'd talked about the tracks they wanted to record, about the producer in Nashville Angela knew. They covered Cathy leaving for Europe in two weeks. What else had they talked about? He'd mentioned he had a new song he wanted to play for her. Was that it?

Didn't matter how it happened, but Angela had gone to the trouble of taking Caroline to her grandmother's house, and she'd made a point of being friendlier when Mark arrived. And now she was asking if Mark had more than music in mind.

All of these thoughts were beginning to coalesce when Angela, a step or two ahead, it seemed, suggested they head to the studio and get started.

Mark sang one of Angela's songs, one she'd written years earlier about a man and his guitar and his dying mother.

"Now I see why you needed a male vocalist," Mark said as he finished a fourth recording. "This gets you right here, doesn't it?" Mark tapped his chest with his fist.

"I hope so," Angela said. "Story songs are a country staple—a good way to get a producer's attention."

"Maybe my voice had too much emotion in it."

"Not too much. Your voice was a perfect fit."

Mark rose from the stool on the recording side of the room and joined Angela by the control board. He stood behind her and rubbed her shoulders, said something about being a good team, and leaned down to kiss the side of her cheek. She reached up and put her hand on top of his. A moment later they embraced. Mark kissed her and she kissed back, then stopped.

"We can work on your song too." She took a deep breath.

Mark instinctively pulled her close again. "What song?" he teased.

Angela laughed. "The song you said you've been working on and finally figured out the chorus. You wanted me to hear it." She paused. "Unless . . . did you have something different in mind?" She nervously glanced around the too-small studio. "The way you were acting on the phone today, I thought . . . I don't know . . . you might ask me something."

Ask her something? Does she think I'm going to propose?

"Tonight? Here?" Mark's voice rose too high on the last word. He shifted his weight and quickly grabbed his sheet music.

A quizzical expression crossed Angela's face before she looked away. "Never mind. I don't know why I said that."

Mark didn't know either. Usually when she brought up engagement, it was to hint about needing to know him for another season. Maybe their conversation at her mother's house had had more of an impact than he realized. But what could he say now? He'd brought some half-written songs. Not the ring.

"I do want to ask what you think of this verse and chorus. Here, let me play a little of it."

"*I'm in love. Can't get enough. Turning me upside down,*" he sang.

"You wrote those words?"

"Yes, I wrote them," Mark said, a bit wounded.

"*When* did you write them?" Angela asked.

Mark hesitated. This was a new song, written for her. But here she was wondering if it was a song he'd written for someone else.

"I started this song in February. For you," Mark said.

A quiet moment ensued. Angela fidgeted with one of the controls, and then she gathered her hair and let it fall across her back.

"Sorry. I didn't mean . . . I don't know what I meant. I like it a lot—the song, the words. They're so sweet."

Mark maneuvered over to where she was again, pulling her in for another hug and kiss. He savored the moment as she snuggled into him. How could he show her that Natalie didn't mean anything to him? Sure, they had dated and he proposed to Natalie, but that was before he'd discovered she was John Jackson's girlfriend. Before he knew she'd been lying to him the entire time. How could he show Angela he loved her and no one else?

"What would be so wrong with proposing here in the studio?" Angela suddenly asked. "You acted like I'd suggested something outrageous earlier."

Mark froze and tried to relax just as quickly. "I wouldn't say this is the most romantic place."

"I don't know why I'm bringing it up. You're reaction surprised me, like there was something wrong."

"Nothing's wrong. At least not anymore. This is a different place than when I brought Natalie to see it. Now that you live here, it's all you," Mark continued rambling, too much and too fast.

Angela stepped back, and her quizzical expression twisted into alarm.

"Wait, what? Natalie was here? How could she? When?" she choked out the words.

Mark's mind raced. What had he said?

"All I meant to say was that I showed Natalie the house when I thought I was going to buy it." He paused.

"You showed her the house and the studio, too? You and she, in here together, with your Realtor?"

"Not exactly. Dave waited upstairs for us. I'd asked him to wait while I . . ."

What was he doing?

"While you what?"

In his effort to not say anything at all, he'd said too much. He looked into Angela's eyes, eyes that teemed with questions and mistrust and pain. He didn't have to answer this. He didn't have to tell her.

But it was too late. And he wasn't going to lie.

"While I proposed," he answered quietly. He began gathering his sheet music, not waiting for a response. The moment was over. Probably the night too. Maybe if he could exit smoothly, they could forget it ever came up.

"Proposed. Here? You didn't even own it. How . . . why would you?"

"Look, I know what it sounds like, and believe me, I don't like reliving one of the stupidest things I've ever done. It was before I knew what she was. Who she was."

"So every time we've worked on our music here, you have *that* memory of her?"

"No, it's not like that."

"Of her saying yes, and then what?"

"And then what? And then nothing. The house was freezing, and Dave was calling for us. Believe me, as proposals go, it was pathetic."

He checked her face for clues. No emotion. That wasn't a good sign.

"What are you thinking? Are you mad at me?" Mark finally asked.

"Don't ask me that right now. I don't know what to think," she said.

"Natalie doesn't mean anything to me. I was wrong and couldn't see who she really was."

"But who you thought she was . . . you proposed to that girl. And who you thought she was . . . that's pretty different from who I am."

"Exactly," Mark said. "Angela, there is no comparison here. I didn't love her . . . I mean, I thought I did."

"Right. I get it. But that's not it." She paused. "I wish you'd told me. I don't know. Maybe that would have helped. This is becoming more than it needs to be. It feels like you were keeping something from me, and that brings up old feelings that don't have anything to do with us."

"When would have been a good time to bring it up?" Mark asked.

"It's fine. We don't have to talk about it anymore."

"It doesn't feel fine," Mark said.

"Maybe if we stop talking about it, it will be." Angela's words cut through Mark.

They both looked around the studio. The melodies and kisses that were in the air a few minutes ago were gone. Mark stood bewildered, staring at the space where five minutes earlier he'd been trying to figure out a way to show Angela he loved *her* and no one else.

Without warning, Angela walked out of the studio and up the stairs.

Mark gathered his things and followed. A heavy-hearted feeling came over him as he left the studio. He was sure they would never use it together again. But he'd built a new studio at the farmhouse for this very reason. Even if Angela had never found out about the proposal to Natalie, he'd planned for them to have a place for making music. He wanted to tell her, to bring her to the farmhouse right now and explain.

She was putting on her coat by the door.

"Thanks for doing the vocal for my song," she said without making eye contact. "I better get going to pick up Caroline. If I'm too late, I'll get questions from my mom."

"Aren't I coming with you?" Mark asked.

Angela didn't respond as she picked up her purse and pulled out her keys. Finally, she met his eyes. "I think I'd rather go alone."

Her words couldn't have hurt more. Mark knew she didn't like to make the drive alone. Any other time—*every* other time—they had gone together. His drive home now felt longer as he wondered what he could have said or done differently.

Once home, he closed the side door behind him and walked through to the new studio.

Will it be enough?

Did he think adding a room would change the way Angela was feeling right now? He'd planned this as a surprise, but he should have told her long ago—to immunize them against the very thing that had happened tonight. There was one thing he hated more than feeling unsure of himself, and that was causing Angela pain.

Papa came around the corner. "Who the devil is there? Mark is that you?"

It took Mark a few seconds to realize he'd walked into the farmhouse, forgetting he'd moved into the cabin.

"Sorry, Papa. Picking up some of my sheet music."

"Land sakes. Everything okay?"

"I'm fine. All good. Sorry to wake you."

"Well, as long as we're both up, maybe it's time for you to learn the second secret."

"Second secret?" Mark asked.

"Have you already forgotten the first?" Papa scrutinized Mark's face. "It begins and ends with love?"

"No, but maybe you're tired."

"I'm awake now." He walked past Mark toward the kitchen. "I'm going to have some warm milk. C'mon and join me."

Mark followed but with regret that he'd come to the house. He was preoccupied with Angela and wasn't sure if this was the best time to learn more from Papa.

After the second swallow of his milk, Papa stared at Mark for a moment. "Bed early, walk early," he said, using a napkin to wipe his mouth.

"You mean wake up early?" Mark asked.

"You have to do that too. But like I said, walk early." Papa insisted.

"That's it?"

"Don't underestimate the power of sleep."

At this moment, Mark began to question if Papa was making up this keeper training on the fly. "Look, I'm sorry for waking you. I might not get to bed as early as you, but I am a little younger," he said, trying to lighten the mood.

"It's not about me anymore. It's about you and the trees. Don't let 'em down, son. Bed early, walk early." Papa eyed Mark before finishing his milk.

Mark drank his milk, but it didn't warm him as much as he hoped. "I don't know. It seems pretty basic—like anyone should follow that advice weather they grow trees or not."

"It's not advice; it's secret number two," Papa said assuredly. "If you follow that pattern well enough, you'll come to understand the timing of things."

Mark waited. "Such as?"

"Everything. When to plant, when to prune. Takes the guesswork outta things, if you're paying attention. Work with the trees. Be in a place where the trees can help you."

"Could it help with relationship timing?" Mark asked, thinking it was a little late now.

"Maybe," Papa said and rubbed his eyes.

"What about fighting MassDOT?"

"I thought you were calling a lawyer for that?"

"I did, but he said there wasn't much we could do until we get an official notice," Mark answered, finishing his milk. "I did come across something, though. What do you think the historical significance is of the farm—maybe the house or cabin?"

"Gotta be something—our Shafer family has been working

this land five—no, make it six, generations," Papa said. Then he announced he was heading to bed. "I'll sleep on it. Remember, your mind has to be healthy, unfettered. And walking early after a good night's rest is the only time you get the trees alone, before the world goes and wakes up and crowds the airwaves. Fight this secret and you put yourself—*and the trees*—at risk."

CHAPTER 7

Angela had lain awake half the night trying *not* to imagine Mark proposing to Natalie. And in the studio! Where she and Mark had spent so much time on their music. *So what if he did?* She argued with herself. *That's over and done, and she's gone.*

She had missed enough sleep that she called Mrs. Shaw and rescheduled their time to paint Christmas village houses—a surprise they'd planned for Caroline.

Caroline! Her mother was likely already on her way to pick her up for the day and wouldn't want to change her Sunday plans. What she wouldn't give for a drive to the beach. Maybe there was time, she could still go.

Angela managed to say very little when she had picked Caroline up last night. It probably peaked Cathy's curiosity about the studio "date" Angela had with Mark, so she rehearsed her answers.

"We had a nice time. No, he didn't propose."

At least not to me!

All her worries were in vain, though. Cathy was otherwise preoccupied.

"We should have planned this better, don't you think?" Cathy said at the door.

"Planned what, Mom?" Angela asked.

"Caroline could have stayed over last night, and that could have saved—"

"Some driving time?" Angela finished her mother's sentence. "Honestly, I didn't think of it until this morning, so thank you for driving out. What do you have planned?"

Caroline skipped out of her room and down the hall. "Shopping," she answered. "Grandma said I can pick out a new backpack for school."

"But you already have one. It's still in decent condition," Angela said.

"Purple and cream was so last year."

Angela looked to her mother only to find her smiling. So much for teaching her daughter to appreciate what she had. She knew the look on her mother's face. That new backpack was as good as bought.

As soon as they left, Angela jumped in her truck and checked the gas gauge.

Should be plenty to get me to Providence and back.

From the moment she learned Mark had proposed to Natalie in the studio, *her* studio, she wanted to get away. Leave her house on Hickory, leave Sutton. Not leave Mark, exactly, but put some space between her and what had happened.

He hadn't done anything wrong. She knew that. He thought he'd loved Natalie, and he'd proposed to her. Just because it happened to be in a room of the house she now owned, why should it matter? Only that they'd been working on music in that room for months and he'd never mentioned it.

But the night had triggered something else. The memory of the hurt and pain she'd suffered when Todd left. That was what—seven years ago? Logically she knew she was overreacting. But she couldn't seem to stop the flood of memories. The only thing that might help was some space.

She turned the truck onto the 295 and checked her watch. She worked out the mental math to make sure she'd be back when her mother and Caroline returned from shopping.

Blue Shutters was probably the farthest beach from Sutton but worth the drive. And, besides, it's what she wanted—distance.

She parked as close as she could without paying for parking, remembering the days she and her friends would walk here with little more than their towels and a few dollars for lunch. Yet these were different days. September was not mid-July, she wasn't sixteen, and she had more weighing her down than an oversized beach towel.

It could have been the clouds and rain casting a dimness on the coast, but the street looked older and the entrance to the beach was more run-down than she remembered. She saw the pavilion and stretch of sand that led to the water. Both looked the same as when she'd walked off the beach every day during those long-ago summers.

But the high-school summer memories were only floating around her mind, much like breezy bubbles might if children were playing nearby. What she came here to remember was a certain night—the night after Todd left.

She had lived through a night and day with no word, no indication of why he hadn't come home. She'd called family, friends, even his not-so-good friends. His band members had been unreachable. She'd scoured her calendar and his belongings to see if she'd missed a scheduled gig. Usually he had a dramatic way of saying good-bye and "Can't wait to see my Angel and my Carol when I get back." She bristled at the memory of those nicknames. But he hadn't left for a gig, and he hadn't said good-bye.

No. When he'd finally called her at eight o'clock at night, he said he was already in Florida. With his lead singer. And he wasn't coming home.

"Even to get your things?" she remembered asking him, rather mindlessly from the shock.

"Just box 'em up for me, babe," he'd said.

She hung up the phone, called her next-door neighbor's teenage daughter to come stay with Caroline once she'd gotten her to sleep, and was out the door.

She'd found a somewhat flat-topped boulder on the far side of the boardwalk, tucked away with some protection from the wind but with a clear view of the ocean. Not that there was anything to see at ten o'clock at night, but she could discern the crashing waves, and staring over the water into a pitch-black horizon comforted her somehow.

Determined not to cry in front of Caroline, she could be alone with her tears here. She could kick the sand and pound the rock, and no one would see. She could wander to the water's edge and wonder about the black depths that stretched on for miles, for lifetimes.

Today, she looked for "her" rock. Not that she'd named it, or carved anything into it, but it had felt like hers ever since it had served as her companion on that dark night—the rock that had waited for her while she'd waded into the water up to her ankles, then to her knees, and then to her chest, until she retreated.

She had sat shivering, knees to her chest, on that rock. A new anger had welled inside her. Never again would she allow someone to get to her the way Todd had. Never again would she let herself be that vulnerable. Caroline needed her. And she needed Caroline.

Now she strolled through the sand with rolled-up jeans and shoes in hand until she found it. She didn't sit on it right away. Rather, she circled it as if she could still see her younger self bracing against a lightless future.

This was why she came. To face this fear, the fear of starting down a path that could end right here again: betrayed, alone, afraid.

Finally she sat on the boulder and rearranged her hair so it would not whip around in front of her face. She dropped her shoes and rubbed her hands on the sides of her legs. The clouds were too thick for any sunlight to emerge. The ocean had a dark and angry motion to it.

Rather unannounced, tears spilled from her eyes. She thought of how grown-up Caroline was now and of how her fears that night for her daughter had been largely unfounded. She didn't try to stop the tears but wiped them gently from her cheeks.

She stood and walked down to the water's edge.

I'm not making the same mistake. This isn't about Mark.

It was the fear that it provoked inside her. A fear she needed to face. Mark was different from Todd in every way he needed to be. And she was different than that nineteen-year-old girl who had been trying to do the right things for the wrong reasons. Or was it the wrong things for the right reasons? Either way, standing on the wet sand, her feet might be cold, but her heart—her heart was at peace. She wrapped her arms around herself and turned her face into the wind, letting her curls fly and bounce about her. The light rain of the morning increased to a steady downpour.

The water curled up around her feet and receded. Once, then twice. With each retreating wave, she let go of the fear.

Climbing into her truck, she used an old towel to wipe the

sand off her feet. When she tried to start the truck, it gave several threatening noises, then finally kicked in.

One of these days, Angela, you'll need a new truck.

The radio came on with a song she hadn't heard in years, one that had inspired her to write several of her favorite songs. She flipped the radio off and drove onto the highway.

Her music. Here she was feeling better about trusting Mark and herself only to have a reminder of the songs she'd written.

Will there be time for songwriting if I'm working at the farm? Will there be room for it?

She saw the exit for Dona Florinda's old neighborhood. How many years had it been? Too many, but for the first year of her lessons, her mother had driven her weekly to Florinda's house. No surprise that after a year of driving, she'd offered a substantial "raise" if Florinda would come to their house instead.

But the weekly trips were nothing like the other lessons. Within a short time, Angela had felt like she was coming home to a place where Florinda and her cousin's family welcomed her in as if *she* were a long-lost cousin.

And that might have been the reason she took the exit. Or maybe it was the old song on the radio. What she wouldn't give to see Florinda, for a chance to talk to her about music.

Her heart raced at the thought. She knew what Florinda would say. She could hear her voice as clear as day. "*Água mole em pedra dura, tanto bate até que fura.*" Something about soft water and a hard rock and not giving up.

But in her English she would follow it by saying, "Don't quit, my Angela. If you don't quit, you will succeed."

She always emphasized the last phrase. "*You* will *succeed.*"

Angela pulled up in front of a group of homes set back from the street far enough to allow for a small lawn and gate. The properties were clean and cared for. Angela turned off her truck and played with the keys in her hand.

She had no reason to believe that Florinda was here. Last she heard she'd returned to Portugal to help her mother. But that had been years ago. And surely she was back in the States. She could be here.

Knocking on the door, Angela felt like she needed to have her piano music in hand. Maybe that was what she would say if her former teacher answered—*I'm here for my lesson.*

Only the door opened and a short, dark-haired man with a mustache stared at her for a moment.

"*Bom dia!*" he said. "Can I help you?"

Angela replied with her best "bon-gee-a."

"I'm looking for a friend. Dona Florinda. Does she still live here?"

The man knitted his eyebrows together. "Not anymore. This was her cousin's house. But they moved." He paused, gathering the words. "Many years ago."

"I see. Sorry to bother you."

The man looked at her thoughtfully. "Wait here." He left the door ajar and disappeared down the hall. Angela had enough time to scold herself for the impulsive stop and for interrupting this man's day.

"Here. This is the number I have for Marguerite, Florinda's cousin. She and her family are still here in Fall River. Try calling. Maybe she can help you."

Angela took the paper, thanked him once in English and once in Portuguese—she hoped—and scurried back to the truck. There was barely enough time to reach home.

She started the truck. Only it didn't quite start. Again, she turned the key. Finally a click.

Stunned that the truck wouldn't start and mad at herself for being stunned, she felt panic constrict her chest. Here she was on the outskirts of Fall River and the truck decides to quit.

Angela called her mother's cell phone. Always a risky venture. She dodged the questions of her exact location and promised to be home by dinner. But there was still the problem of getting herself and the truck home.

I'll give it a little more time and try again.

Every ten minutes she attempted to start the truck, exercising some hope—but mostly stubbornness—that the starter had one more turn in it.

Forty-five minutes later, at the point she would either need to pay roadside assistance to come or call Mark, a man emerged from a house across the street and started toward his black Hummer. Before getting in, he stared at Angela and the truck. She immediately took interest in something in her purse, but when she tucked her hair behind her ear and looked out of the corner of her eye, he was approaching.

"Are you having some trouble?"

Wearing a dress shirt and tie, he wasn't as worrisome as she was prepared for him to be. Regardless, this was going to be a job for roadside.

"It's my starter. I think it finally quit."

"How about I make a call and help you get to where you need to be."

"That's nice of you, but I do have coverage on my plan."

"You don't want to wait here all night, do you?"

No, I do not.

He was already calling.

"Listen," she tried to get his attention. "You don't have to do that."

"My brother owns a tow truck. You sure?"

"That's kind of you, but I'm good," she bluffed.

She searched farther in her purse for her insurance card and the roadside number.

"Are you close to home? I can give you a lift."

Angela assessed his shirt and tie and the black hummer. Nothing dangerous, exactly. But then, most people with ill-intent didn't wear a sign on their foreheads, did they?

"Not close, no—Sutton." She closed her mouth, not happy about disclosing where she lived, but she felt the need to prove it was too far for him to help her.

"Sutton? I've done business there. Lots of trees," he said with a faraway look in his eye, and then his phone rang.

This gave Angela time to look more closely for the number. She found it and began dialing. He ended his call and started his conversation with her without missing so much as a preposition.

Angela looked over his features and receding hairline and wondered how old he might be. His posture added inches to his height, and he spoke with his hands.

Meanwhile, the representative on the phone was asking for her information. She began answering the questions. The man outside her truck began asking her what she did for work and how long she had lived in Sutton, and had she ever been to the tree farm there?

Due to her divided attention, she inadvertently divulged more personal information than she wanted to. Couldn't he see she was on the phone?

"I'm sorry, I've got to go—" she was saying to the man, only the roadside rep thought she was talking to him and hung up.

"Sure. If you think you're okay here," the man in the shirt and tie said, but he still hadn't walked away. "You know, I'll be in Sutton next weekend, Friday. How about dinner?"

Angela realized the roadside rep had hung up at the same time she was being asked out.

Seriously?

"Here's my card. Give me a call or I'll call you. There's a steakhouse in Millbury."

She took the card out of pure exasperation.

If this will get him to leave . . .

"Name's John." He walked away from her truck, his cell phone ringing as he headed for his Hummer.

She looked at his card before tossing it onto the passenger seat.

John Jackson, Developer.

She didn't stop to think if the name sounded familiar. She only looked at the time—3:00 p.m., and knowing her mother, she'd want an early dinner.

She called the roadside number again. While listening to hold music, she tapped her steering wheel and had the thought to start the truck one more time.

To her complete shock, it worked.

She navigated the streets out of Florinda's former neighborhood and to the highway, resisting the urge to speed to be sure she didn't run out of gas.

Had that man really asked her to dinner? Well, she was not available. Not next weekend, not any weekend.

CHAPTER 8

Mark lifted the lid on the dusty box they had found last Christmas. A smile curved up one side of his mouth as he remembered that day—the dinner, the search, and finding the box. And kissing Angela. Briefly, but still.

He found the ring inside, where it had remained after Angela had given it back. Of course she'd done it playfully. And he had no reason to believe she wouldn't accept it as an engagement ring, but he needed to know more about it.

He held the ring up to the light streaming through the side window. It needed a good cleaning, but the diamonds themselves were all in place. He rubbed it against his sleeve, counted the five stones, and slid it over his pinky.

Maybe he should consult a jeweler first. Was it his great-grandmother's ring? Or her grandmother's ring?

There was a knock on the cabin door. Papa opened it, not waiting for Mark to answer. He moved a bit quicker these days. Mark was sure it had something to do with Mrs. Shaw.

"Watcha got there?" Papa asked.

Mark closed the lid and curled his hand around the ring. "Just checking on what we found in this box last year." He eyed Papa for a moment, then uncurled his hand and held up the ring.

"Any idea who wore this ring, Papa?"

"It wasn't your nana. I can tell you that much. As for my mother, I can't say I remember. Never occurred to me now that we're talking about it."

"So it could be her ring?"

Papa stepped closer to Mark, carefully took the ring from his hand, and held it close to his good eye. "I 'spose so, but then again she lived longer than my father—so she would have been the one to put it in the box. Seems strange."

"So maybe it's her mother's ring?"

"This is important to you, then?" Papa seemed frustrated by the fruitless questions.

"Never mind. I'll figure it out. I'd like to know if I'm giving Angela an antique or not."

"Go have it appraised. What could that hurt?" he said and handed the ring back.

"I'm headed over to the jewelers soon. Would you like to come with me?" Mark asked.

"Now that's a good idea. I may need to look at their selection," he said.

When they left the farm, Papa was quiet. Though not unusual for him, he did seem less cheerful.

"Is there something on your mind?" Mark asked.

"As a matter of fact, there is. You getting the ring looked at answers my first question. You're getting serious about asking her. Do you know when the wedding will be?"

Mark stared over the two-lane asphalt road. "I guess I haven't thought that far ahead. At this point, I'm hoping she'll say yes."

When they arrived at the jewelers, Mark explained what he knew about the ring while Papa started browsing.

Once they were alone in the showroom, Papa picked up their conversation from the drive. "Why don't you think she'll say yes?"

Mark didn't want to relive the other night, but here they were.

"She found out I proposed to Natalie—in her studio."

"I see," Papa said without much expression.

"I'm thinking if I plan a nice night, something memorable, she will forget about Natalie."

"I see."

"Isn't that a good idea?" Mark asked.

Papa was gazing at rings, his leathery hands resting on top of the glass case. He seemed in no hurry to answer.

"Why do you think Natalie is the problem? You may want to apologize for not telling Angela sooner," he said without looking up. "This one's a beauty. Bet the price is too."

"Honestly, what could I have said?" Mark asked.

"Have you told her about the MassDOT project—what they're planning to do?" Papa asked.

"No. I mean not yet," Mark stammered. "I will. I planned to tell her when I got it worked out."

"Mm-hmm."

"What does that mean?"

"It means if you love this girl, you'll have to figure out a way to talk to her. I don't know too many girls who like feeling left out. Seems to me it's the point of being a couple. Sharing things." Papa stood straighter and shook his head, then he dropped into a chair next to one of the displays.

Mark *had* planned on telling her, but Papa was right. Angela definitely liked it when he shared things with her. Sooner than later. He would rather give her good news about the farm, though, not present a problem. And he didn't want anything overshadowing the proposal. What he knew for sure was he wanted to share the farm life, the work and rewards, with someone. And he wanted it to be her.

He crossed the room and sat next to Papa. "Thanks for coming with me."

"Glad you asked. I'll need to check my savings. Been some time since I've been in a place like this. Are those prices as high as I think they are? Can I tell the fellow I don't want to buy the store, only one little ring?" Papa asked.

Mark chuckled, and then it hit him. "Wait. Do you want to give the ring from the box to Mrs. Shaw? I'm sorry, I shouldn't have assumed I could take it."

"Nonsense. You found it with Angela," Papa said.

"And Caroline," Mark said. "She's the one that saw the box in the wall. But would you rather the ring go to Mrs. Shaw?" Mark asked.

"Dorothy. Her name's Dorothy. And like I said, you found it. You give it to Angela," Papa insisted.

Mark wasn't sure he'd ever heard Mrs. Shaw's name, but clearly that was what Papa wanted to call her from now on.

"Here we are. You've got a fascinating little ring. I bet you're anxious to finally know more about it," the jeweler said as he came back into the showroom.

"Actually, we're pressed for time," Mark said.

"We are?" Papa asked.

Mark had just noticed his watch. If he was going to reserve the Sutton gazebo, he needed to get over to the town hall before they closed.

"If it's all there in the paperwork, I'll take it and look it over later," Mark said, sitting on the edge of his seat. "I've got some business to take care of in town," he said to Papa.

The man's smile dropped, and he raised his eyebrows. "You don't want to hear about it?" the man asked.

"I do," Papa said.

Mark looked at the ring as the man held it in a new box. Cleaned and sitting against the black interior, it sparkled with a new shine.

"Sure, what can you tell me?" Mark asked.

"First, let me say this ring is in great condition. I'd be hard-pressed to believe anyone ever wore it. If she did, she babied it so well there aren't the normal wear-and-tear scratches."

"So that's the good news? Does that mean there's bad news?" Mark asked.

"No, no. Nothing like that. The diamonds are genuine, the gold is high quality. I can describe it in more detail, but you mentioned you're short on time," the appraiser said. He did sit down, though, pausing a moment before finally sharing what Mark was convinced would be bad news.

"This ring isn't as old as you thought it might be. What were you guessing? Late 1800s, early 1910s, or '20s? Don't be disappointed." He took the ring out of the box and held it up, turning it. He handed it to Mark as he continued to describe it.

"From what we can tell—I had a couple of the guys take a look—we'd say this ring was made somewhere around 1960, probably 1965—give or take a few years."

1965? Mark had never considered the ring so new. Even though it wasn't new. But how could it be? Whose could it be? Slowly he looked at the ring and then at the appraiser, and a new question formed in his mind.

Papa asked it before he could.

"Could it have been made around 1969?"

"Certainly." The appraiser sat back in his chair.

Mark put the ring in the case, stared at it for a second, then closed the lid and stood up. "Never been worn, you said?"

Papa stood too.

"Not enough to show. Looks like you have an idea where it came from," the appraiser said expectantly.

They spoke simultaneously.

"My son," Papa said.

"My dad," Mark said.

They weren't making a lot of sense, and the appraiser had a right to wear a confused look on his face. But Mark thanked him instead of explaining any further.

"We better get going."

"Wait, don't you want to know the value?"

"I already do!" Mark said.

On his way to the town hall, Mark brought Papa back to the farm. Neither was expecting the ring to be the one Mark's dad had bought. But that explained why it had never been worn. It wasn't his mother's ring—it was Cathy's. Most likely the ring his dad had bought for Cathy and had never been able to give her.

"I told you that ring was meant for you," Papa said.

"Meant for Angela," Mark said. He couldn't wait to tell her. Thursday. He could propose on Thursday and tell her the whole story.

"Now, I've got work to do," Papa said as they approached the farm. He put his hand on the truck's door handle.

"What work is that?" Mark asked.

"I don't think you and Angela want to take up residence in the cabin any more than Dorothy and I do. Seeing as you didn't build another master, I'll need to find a place for us to live," he said as he climbed out of the truck.

Mark watched him go and waited a minute before he drove off. How could he have known Papa was going to get married? And this soon? Of course, they weren't engaged yet either. Papa still had to ask Mrs. Shaw. But why did Mark's engagement and hopefully soon-to-be wedding have to mean Papa had to move?

What if Mrs. Shaw said no? Or wasn't interested in getting married at all? Papa could move back to the cabin. He enjoyed a moment of relief at the thought that maybe there was a chance he wasn't putting his grandfather out of his home.

He drove away from the farmhouse, and as he turned the corner he remembered Caroline and the trees she'd picked out for Christmas—not one but two. And Papa's teasing words. *Love matches and weddings before Christmas.*

Could it be?

The Sutton town hall closed at four, and not that he couldn't go another day, and not that he thought the gazebo was in such high demand, but the idea of proposing there had grown on him, and he wanted that part of the plan in place.

The rush he felt wore off as he approached the town square. The speed limit put everyone at a crawl, and buildings and the common left him feeling like he'd driven back in time fifty years or more. In fact, it set Mark to wondering if any of the land or these buildings were on the National Register. And if they were, what would that have to do with his farm? Someone in Sutton had to know how to put a landmark on the list.

He walked up steps guarded by four white columns and in through the doors to find an unattended reception desk. A fan was on in the corner of the office, blowing a stream of air over the desks and rustling papers.

A sign read "Ring bell for service." Mark waited, rocking on his heels before he hit the bell. It was loud, and though he didn't know who or what to expect, nothing happened. He walked around the entryway, read some notices on the bulletin board, and saw some brochures for the fire department. A paper pinned to the board caught his eye—"Volunteers needed at the Sutton Historical Society."

"Can I help you?" a woman's voice called from behind him.

He turned and stepped over to the desk. "I'm hoping you can. Who do I talk to about reserving the gazebo?"

"That's Pete," she said, waving a fly away. She sat down at her desk and held up her reading glasses as she peered at a file. Her hair was short and dyed brown over gray. She wore a clip that kept if off her face.

"And how do I reach him?" he asked after an awkward pause.

"Pete's out of town. Granddaughter's wedding."

Mark waited to see if she would offer an alternative.

"You can come back next week. He should be in after the twenty-sixth, I suspect." She put the file down and smiled pleasantly, but it seemed only because she was supposed to.

"Actually, I'd like to reserve the gazebo for this Thursday, the twenty-second, if I could."

"Well, you could if Pete were here, and no one else has it, and you fill out his application and put a deposit down. We didn't used to require deposits, you know. Seeing how it's free for residents. But ever since the Silver Sneakers Club used it for a social—and a few of their walkers tore up the floor—we've started requiring a deposit."

Mark blinked.

"But since Pete isn't here, I guess you'll have to change your plans."

Mark opened his mouth to speak but closed it. She stared at him rather unapologetically. Finally, he made a last attempt.

"Look, it's the autumnal equinox, and I know that isn't the most important day of the year, but it is to me and my girlfriend."

"Do I know your girlfriend?"

Mark thought this was an odd question, as she didn't even know Mark, but so far everything about this conversation had been odd.

"I'm not sure—her name is Angela . . . Donovan." He waited as she thought about it. "She moved here a few years ago."

"Hmm, no. Doesn't ring a bell. But you, you look like—do I know your brother Ben?"

"I don't have a brother. Just a sister who moved to California," Mark said, not sure how this was helping.

"Give me a second. What's your name?"

"Mark Shafer," he said cautiously, though not sure why.

"Shafer! You're Greg and Janey's son! You wouldn't know me, but I went to school with your mom and dad. I'm sorry, honey. You must miss them. I heard about that awful fire. I'm so sorry."

Mark cleared his throat. "Thank you. It's okay," he reassured her as best he could. "About Pete and changing my plans—I was hoping I could propose there Thursday night and wanted to make sure I didn't have to compete with anyone else. Like the Silver Sneakers."

"A proposal? Why didn't you say so?" She hopped up from her chair and scurried over to another desk, maybe Pete's, and returned with a binder. She produced a sheet of paper for Mark and then thumbed through the pages.

"Fill that out. I'm going to go ahead and waive that deposit. It's only twenty-five dollars. If it's just the two of you, I trust you won't be doing any damage to the property. And let me see here. Wait, you said this Thursday?" She looked up at Mark with crestfallen eyes. "Oh, sweetie, the Astronomy Club reserved it a month ago. Starting an hour after sunset. So what's that—about seven thirty or eight?"

Mark held his pen on the address line of the application. *The Astronomy Club?*

"You know what? Don't tell anyone Miss Lila told you this. You and your girl come right out there to that Gazebo, and you pop that question. Do you think you can manage it before seven thirty? Worst case is you'll have an audience of some retired men with telescopes, but if you get there early enough, I bet you'll be just fine."

"Before seven thirty it is," Mark said, though it didn't seem like he had much choice in the matter.

She pulled the application from his hands as he finished signing it and chatted away about Pete and how she knew he wouldn't mind her helping Greg Shafer's son.

Thankful the gazebo and the common wasn't going to be overridden with a larger event or group, Mark thanked Miss Lila and headed for the door. The bulletin board caught his eye and he remembered . . .

"Do you know anything about the Historical Society? Who would I talk to about having some land listed on the register?" he asked. She was putting the binder back on the other desk.

"That's Pete, too," she said.

Thinking of their exchange over the gazebo, Mark thought it best if he came back and actually talked to Pete. "Thanks. I'll track him down next week, like you said."

"Sure, you could do that." She returned to her chair and began arranging papers. "Or you could call Mrs. Simmons. Pete would just give you her number anyway."

A sudden clap of thunder broke over their heads, and rain began to pour against the back windows of the building, furiously pelting the thick panes.

"Darn! I was hoping to get home before the roads turned into rivers," Miss Lila said with a scowl.

"Do you by chance have her number?"

"Of course I do."

"Wait, did you say Mrs. Simmons? The same one who taught eighth-grade English?"

"That's her—and good, you already know her. That will help. She can be a little . . . what would you say . . . fussy? But you won't have to worry about that if she knows you. You won't have half the battle everyone else does."

With that, she handed Mark the number on a slip of paper that he tucked into his wallet.

He walked out of the town hall's double doors into the pouring rain inundated with memories of his eighth-grade English class and Mrs. Simmons. A teacher who didn't share his sense of humor or "lack of respect for deadlines," as she called them.

Forget half the battle. I'll probably have double.

CHAPTER 9

Angela arrived at the Blackstone apartments' rental office to meet the new hire. It had taken months, nine and a half months, but they'd finally found a replacement. Home office would handle the training but had asked Angela to handle a bit of general orientation. A tour and a few tips. "She mentioned that if you went to lunch with her that would be enough," Gloria from the home office had said. "But she may need a little more help than that."

She opened the door to a squeal from across the room.

"Eeeek! Angela? Angela Elliott. Is that you?" The new hire bounced over to Angela with both arms outstretched. Before Angela could dodge her, she was grabbed by the shoulders and kissed on each cheek.

Ashley Porter? Still as dramatic as high school.

"It's me," Angela said after awkwardly extracting herself from Ashley's enthusiastic greeting.

Though I haven't used the Elliott name for a while.

As if she could read minds, Ashley continued. "You don't use Elliott, though. Wait, wait . . . don't tell me. It will come to me. You married the guy in your band. You really had a band, didn't you? How long had you known him, two months? Three? Todd—

73

that was his name, and he was hot too. Though that didn't help so much with your mom. She would have preferred no looks to some sort of title, right? And Todd, he um . . . what instrument did he play? Donovan! That's the name. I remembered because the same month you married him, we hired a new chef with the same last name. No relation, of course, but yeah. So you're still Angela Donovan? No ring on your finger, I see."

No ring. That was true. And that was Ashley—three insults per breath as usual.

Was she seriously the new manager at Blackstone?

Doing something she wouldn't normally do, Angela checked Ashley's left hand. Sure enough, a fairly obscene diamond rested there. But something didn't add up. Namely the man Ashley married had much too much money and even more pride for his wife to be taking up residence as manager of the Blackstone, no matter how quaint the apartments were.

"I kept Donovan. It's my daughter's name, too," Angela said simply. "So, wow, it's a surprise to see you here. I mean what brings you to Sutton?" Before Ashley could answer, Angela looked at her ring again. *She brought it up first.* "How's your husband?"

"My what? Oh, you mean Willard? We are so done. Divorce final—like almost a year. Okay, like three months. But we separated long before that. I am so over him. Over all of it."

Angela wasn't sure what *that* meant, but this concerned her even more. If that ring was from someone new, that would mean it would be all she'd hear about over lunch. Lunch! Did she, like seriously, have to survive lunch with Ashley?

I'm already sounding like her!

"Sorry to hear that," Angela said as she fiddled with her purse. "It's almost lunchtime. Did you want to go grab a bite to eat?"

"I'm so glad you asked. Yes, I'm starved. Did you keep a mini fridge in the office here? I couldn't find one, so I thought maybe you had one but took it with you, which I could totally understand if it was stainless or maybe special order. So I'll need to know where the POs are, right? Purchase orders—I've learned that. I'll fill one of those out pronto for a fridge and probably a microwave. I don't see why they couldn't put a wall up over there and create like a mini kitchen, you know? I could stock it with protein bars and maybe some acai berries. I've heard Oprah used those to lose weight. That will need to be project number one."

They were in the restaurant, seated and halfway through their salads before Ashley stopped midsentence and announced how inconsiderate she'd been to not ask Angela what was happening in her life.

"I know you have Caroline, but you do get out, right? I mean, there has to be some kind of a social life in Sutton. How long have you lived here?"

Was she kidding? That had been one of the things Angela liked about Sutton—the lack of social life or, rather, the lack of social*ites*.

"It's been a couple years now. I was looking for something that wasn't Providence. I hang out in the country." Angela held in a smirk. "Some of the best people I've ever met live here."

"The country? I hadn't thought of that. I mean, I know we're not in Providence anymore, but I was hoping you and I, well, you could introduce me to some friends. You know, help me get settled. I can't be all about the apartments. We know the tenants won't be my friends."

Angela clanged her fork inadvertently—or not. "I can introduce you to one of my good friends." She ate another bite of spinach and chewed slowly. "Her name is Dorothy Shaw. She may be getting engaged soon."

"She sounds like my kind of girl. I mean, that's exactly what I mean. Don't let this ring fool you. I'm sure it didn't. You knew I was divorced, right? I only wear it to fend off the non-salaried. Believe me, I take this off faster than my cucumber-facial scrub when there are suits in the room under forty."

Same old Ashley.

"Let's see. Dorothy—she's in her late sixties. I've never asked her, but she has grandchildren. And her boyfriend, he's in his seventies and helps run a farm. Don't see him wearing a suit much. But you'll probably meet her soon enough. She lives in 312. Always pays her rent on time, if not a day early."

Ashley's jaw hung agape. "I'll . . . keep my eye out."

Sometime during their lunch, Ashley's chatter ranged from shallow to probing to awkwardly intimate. There were moments where Angela glimpsed a few emotions flit across her face. She was always trying to be someone she wasn't, though who she was—pretty and energetic with a knack for detail—could have been enough. Aside from trying to be more, better, best, she seemed to have a kind of ache, an aura of loneliness. She had friends to fit her shopping and gossip habits but not even one friend to turn to when life stopped moving along to the snap of her fingers. Building a façade for a life to impress one's closest friends made it hard to turn to them when that façade came crashing down.

It was beginning to make sense why she'd chosen a job in Sutton. And why she wore a place-holder ring.

Angela ignored the pointed though unintended insults. She waded through the verbal debris and passed up the too-numerous opportunities to pass judgment or point out the girl's mistakes. Ashley may have been a master of pretense and an expert of image-making, but pain was pain, and Angela knew that no amount of claiming she was "over all of it" could hide it. At least not from Angela.

And that may have been the reason she heard herself agree to bring Ashley to the farm.

Angela paced by the fireplace at the front of the farmhouse, her eyes darting to the bay window and back to the clock. Inviting Ashley to visit Shafer Farm seemed like the right thing to do at the time. Maybe not the right thing, but maybe the compassionate thing. Problem was, now Angela couldn't find a compassionate bone in her body.

What was I thinking?

All Ashley will see is Donna's barn and holiday crafts, not Gucci. Trees were the main attraction, not men in suits. The farm did have the Shafer family, namely Mark. But that was sort of the last thing Angela wanted to show Ashley.

What could she do about it now? One more look at the clock and it was too late. She saw her pull up, close the door—and what was that? A Mazda Miata? She was wearing boots, *high-heeled* boots. Leggings and a skirt? Could it even be called a skirt?

I've had bigger dinner napkins.

Angela sighed and checked the side door. No sign of Mark. That was a good thing. She could greet Ashley and talk for a bit, let her adjust to what would surely feel like a foreign country.

Another minute went by but no knock on the door. Angela stepped to the window and couldn't find her at first. How odd. How could she get lost from the car to the door?

Then she saw the corner of Ashley's shoulder off to the east side of the porch and then her hair flip. Twice. Angela craned her neck a little farther toward the edge of the window.

Who was she talking to?

"Any closer and you might fall in," Papa said as he entered the room.

She's not talking to Papa.

"Watcha lookin' at?" he asked as he moseyed over to the window.

"Waiting for my friend."

"You mean the one with the fancy shoes out there talking to Mark?"

Now Angela could see them in full view, Mark walking casually toward the door listening to Ashley, who was talking and bobbing and flipping her hair. If she meant it as a subtle flirtation, it was fast becoming a nervous tick.

Angela scanned Mark's face and his body language for clues. Was he put off? Surprised? Interested? No, of course not. But there were no clues. He looked like his genuine self, listening, walking, with an easy smile on his face.

Knots formed in Angela's stomach. *What have I done?*

She moved quickly from the window as they approached the porch, though she didn't have quite enough time to get involved in something other than straightening pictures on the fireplace mantel. *Great.*

Mark opened the door, allowing Ashley to enter ahead of him.

"Angela! There you are." She moved directly to Angela for a hug, or cheek kiss, or whatever it was that she did, her heeled boots clacking against the floor as she walked.

Angela caught Mark's eye over Ashley's shoulder. He wore a smile punctuated by raised eyebrows. All Angela could do was plead with her eyes.

"You didn't tell me the farm was so quaint, Angela. Or that it was this far out of the way. I mean where is the nearest drugstore? What do you do if you run out of mascara? Not that I buy mine there, of course, but in a pinch I can grab some Revlon and no one knows the difference. But seriously. I thought it would be a *little* bit country. You didn't tell me you were roughing it."

An awkward pause ensued. Before Angela could respond to not ever needing emergency mascara, Ashley continued.

"And you also didn't tell me I'd be meeting the owner of the farm." With those words, her attention shifted deliberately to Mark with another signature flip of her hair.

Angela acted quickly at that move, working her way to Mark's side. She stopped short of resting her hand on his arm, mainly to appear much calmer than she was.

"So sorry. I thought for sure I told you," she offered, though as she said the words she knew she hadn't had the chance. "Mark, this is my friend from Providence, Ashley." She hesitated a moment at the last name, not sure which name Ashley was using.

"Oh, we've met. I even got a little tour from the parking lot to the porch. The hand-carved door is exquisite. Mark is going to find the name of the craftsman for me."

Met and started a research project together. In less than thirty yards.

"I'm sure we have a file somewhere. All I know is that it wasn't mass produced. My mother loved originals."

Ashley had locked eyes with Mark and stood there as if she were soaking up every word he spoke. Had Angela not been standing so close to him, she may have felt like she wasn't even in the room.

Say something, anything, to break the spell.

"Couldn't you call your mom and ask? I mean, a woman never forgets a good designer," Ashley rattled off, now glancing about the room, seeing it for the first time.

Mark looked at Angela. An "I'm-sorry" expression was all she could offer. This was going from bad to worse. And they weren't even through the introductions.

"My mother passed away when I was ten." He said it reverently but also unaffectedly. Angela recognized the kindness in his eyes, always present when he spoke of his mother.

"Oh, I didn't know. I'm so sorry."

"Why don't I show you the rest of the house," Angela said. Turning to Mark, she added, "Maybe we could catch up with you by Donna's barn in a half an hour?"

"Sounds good."

Angela waited for Mark to leave, but he paused for a moment, perhaps only recognizable to her. Then, without warning, he put his arm around Angela's waist, pulled her against him, and kissed her cheek—ever so close to her lips. Brief but deliberate. And conveniently on the side facing Ashley.

As Mark left the room, Angela rode the wave of momentary thrill and turned to face Ashley, bracing herself for the inquisition.

"What was that? No, don't tell me. Seriously, that was a kiss. Okay, more than a kiss because I saw his arm go around your waist. Like . . . are you two . . . ? Don't tell me. I mean, you didn't tell me you're . . . you're dating him! Dating, right? How long has this been going on? And by going on I mean—"

"Let me stop you right there." Angela took a breath deep enough for the two of them. "We're not engaged." Angela held up her hand, and an anticlimactic quiet settled over them.

Ashley appeared both disappointed and somewhat pleased in a single facial expression.

"Yet. We're not engaged *yet*," Angela added. She might have been imagining the pleased look, but just in case she wasn't.

Ashley and her heeled boots clacked over to the dining room, and she offered a little laugh.

"Now I know why you wanted me to come to the farm. This is going to be your home." She said it simply enough, but Angela wasn't sure if there were an edge in there somewhere.

"No, remember you asked about Sutton. Meeting people."

"Uh-huh. This is lovely Angela, it is." At this, her tone shifted noticeably. As she walked to the kitchen, leading a kind of self-tour, she pointed to the area walled off with plastic. "What's happening there?" she asked.

"Mark is expanding," Angela said, hoping that would satisfy her since she didn't know more than that. When Mark had started the construction, he'd declared it a surprise until it was done.

"Nice. Maybe a modern master bedroom suite for the two of you?"

Before Angela could admit to not knowing, Ashley expertly changed the subject, or at least breathlessly. Now in the kitchen, she commented on everything from the cabinets to the angle of light from the windows. "At least your future, uh, *late* mother-in-law had good taste. What about your father-in-law? Does he still own the house?"

Tact. Did she have any?

"He died in a fire with Mark's mom," Angela said. Before Ashley could reply, Angela changed the subject and stammered out some words. "How about we head outside. The trees are spectacular," Angela said while motioning to the window. She saw a bit of wistfulness on Ashley's face. "This time of day," she continued, "the angle of the light, like you were mentioning. It's gorgeous here."

As they approached Donna's craft barn, Mark was waiting. Angela loved how tall he stood near the door with his square shoulders and tousled brown hair against the red of the barn wall, the white of the door trim. A familiar emotion flitted through her, that longing to be in his arms.

Then she remembered Ashley and how this was her first time at the farm. Was it her first time on *any* farm? Not that Angela wanted to read her mind. The thought of that was exhausting, but what *was* she thinking?

Angela looked again at the trees, at the barn, and at Mark. Did the barn need a new coat of paint? Was the fading sunlight doing the trees justice?

Was Mark as rugged-looking as she thought? Or just rough around the edges?

Angela pushed the thoughts aside as Mark greeted them.

"Hi, Mark. Angela didn't tell me she had her very own Tarzan."

Angela cringed—*Tarzan? This isn't the jungle!*

Ashley spoke full speed ahead. Angela hoped Mark had missed the reference completely. She should have warned Mark about her, the inadvertent put-downs, but they were always reserved for her, she'd thought. Angela didn't think she'd aim any at Mark.

Ashley couldn't have meant it the way it sounded, could she? She was already commenting on the slant of the ground and how had she *known* she'd be hiking she would have worn her Stuart Weitzmans.

"I've never had a reason to take them out of the box, and I promised myself I would, you know, go hiking one day so I wouldn't be haunted by the $500 price tag. I mean I could have waited for a sale, but Weitzmans are ridiculous that way. I would have never found my size. You'd think five and a half would be so easy to find. It's the half size—I mean why did my feet have to grow just enough to take half the joy out of shoe shopping?"

Whatever compassion Angela may have felt at their now-too-distant lunch, she was losing over Ashley's great trial in life—that of an impractical shoe size.

There were no designer hiking boots for sale in the barn. Though that didn't stop Ashley from suggesting it.

"Donna's barn, what a nice touch. You know, though, everyone can see it's a barn. Add the word *boutique* and voilà, you can sell to an entirely new market."

Donna's Barn Boutique?

Angela would have to think about that one.

Mark ventured a word or two. "Can't say that Donna was much of a boutique woman."

After Ashley left, Mark and Angela walked through the back lot of trees from the barn to the front lot. The setting sun glowed over the western horizon. The trees stood as darkened sentinels.

Angela sighed, displaying obvious relief. Not that she didn't still worry what Mark might have thought of Hurricane Ashley having just moved through the farm. Could she declare how she didn't want to think, look, or act like Ashley in any way without being a miserable friend? Had Mark gotten to know her well enough over these last eight or nine months to know the difference?

"So you and Ashley—friends?"

"High school friends—the loosest meaning of that word."

"And now?" Mark asked guardedly.

"She's the new manager of Blackstone. But my time there is done. I only invited her here because she's new to Sutton, and she says she's over her divorce, but I don't know. She may be needier than ever."

"And?"

"And what? That's all."

"You don't think she'll be wanting to hang out, do some girls' nights?"

At this, Angela felt even more relieved. If all Mark was worried about was Angela spending time with Ashley—well, that was not going to happen.

"She may want to, but I don't have the wallet or stomach for the kind of shopping she does."

Mark reached for Angela's hand. The warmth of his touch distracted her for a moment and left her unprepared for what he would say next.

"It's not too late to tell me if this isn't going to work out. I saw the way Ashley looked at the trees and the house. I get it. I've seen it before. If it hadn't been for the hand-carved door, she might have made up a reason to leave before we even made it to the porch."

Angela continued walking, speechless, her mind replaying the last hour.

"I always worried it would be a stretch. Us . . . you . . . the farm," he said next.

His tone of defeat tugged at Angela's heart. No, it pierced it. She wanted to protest but shock choked her words.

Mark continued. "This isn't Providence. And I'm not Tarzan."

What did he mean, "It would be a stretch"?

Angela could hardly see the road for all her indignation.

The nerve he has to say such a thing.

She tried taking a deep breath or two but felt far too hypocritical doing it. *I don't want to cool down. I want to stay mad. At least until I can figure out why his oh-so-considerate offer makes me so angry.*

At that, she thought of his words again. *"It's not too late to tell me if this isn't going to work out."*

Why isn't it too late? Do you feel so little for me?

The road curved before her exit. She narrowly missed another car while changing lanes. She forced another breath for her own safety's sake.

"I always worried it would be a stretch," he'd said. *"Us . . . you . . . the farm."*

He'd included *farm* like it was part of the "us" he talked about. Of course it was a part of them. The lack of confidence in his voice, the sound of resignation she heard—like he was less surprised and mostly deflated. If he'd been that skeptical, why let it go on this long?

Is this why he hasn't proposed? Did he ever think I could fit in?

"This isn't Providence," he'd said. Only there wasn't defensiveness in his voice. He'd said it plain and proud. Angela had left Providence a long time ago, in more ways than one. And never cared to go back. Still, his words felt as much like a rejection as anything could.

Doesn't he know I love him?

Tears spilled over her cheeks. Angela swiped at them with an impatient disgust.

Useless tears.

Not wanting to admit her anger was a cover for sadness yet, she hit the accelerator as she approached her house.

"*I'm not Tarzan,*" he had declared.

Well, I'm not Jane, she thought. *And I'm not Ashley Porter.*

CHAPTER 10

Mark didn't watch Angela leave. What was there to see? Another hope that wouldn't work out? He walked up the porch steps, heard her start the truck. It sputtered. He paused, but the engine engaged, then the wheels crunched over the gravel. He opened and closed the hand-carved door behind him. No reason to make it harder than it was.

Had he been fooling himself? Like he had with Natalie? Seeing what he wanted to see, instead of the obvious? Not that Angela was anything like Natalie or Ashley, but how could someone accustomed to so much money and comfort be happy at the farm?

She said she was. She even said she would be.

How long would it be before she realized it wouldn't get any more exciting?

Mark walked to the cabin, pulled out his guitar, pushed some boxes he'd brought over, and started strumming, automatically playing Angela's song. Only instead of lifting his mood, it worsened it. He changed the chords. He changed the words and put down the guitar. Nothing helped.

He wandered over to Donna's barn and surveyed the room. Mrs. Shaw had taken the shelving down and rearranged the floor plan. Now it was shopper-friendly, with new endcap spaces for larger displays. And the cash register had been moved to the side of the large room, giving customers more merchandise to look at while they stood in line.

All good changes.

What the barn didn't have was Donna. Mark wanted to find her with a box of new craft supplies. He would have offered to help unpack it, pretending to know what she did with all that wire, glue, and beads. He would have been able to ask her about Angela and what he should do.

Mark walked through the newly designed area until he reached the back of the room. On the wall next to her favorite window hung Donna's picture in a craft frame she'd made herself.

He didn't often pause here. He didn't linger over her memory, at least not in the barn where it had the power to overwhelm him.

The barn door opened, startling Mark. Papa brushed the rain from his arms as he walked in.

"Thought it might be you. Saw the light on from my place and knew it wasn't Dorothy."

"I'm checking—uh, looking at—the new layout. Mrs. Shaw's done a lot of work here."

"This time a' night?" Papa scratched the back of his head. "Looks to me like you're lovesick," he said with some frustration. No smile, no gentle laugh.

"I wouldn't call it that."

"Doesn't matter what ya call it. The only cure for it is asking her to marry ya, and the sooner the better."

Somehow having this conversation with Papa wasn't nearly the same as having it with Donna. Mark turned on his heel, taking in the scope of the room, and let his eyes catch Donna's smile. She was getting a good laugh at this, he was sure.

"It's not like that, Papa. I'm worried she might not end up liking the farm as much as she thinks she will."

"That so?" Papa walked to the back, closer to Mark, and pulled out one of the register stools. "This have anything to do with her friend showin' up and prancing around?"

"Maybe. I don't know."

"Angela seems like she knows her mind. She's had plenty of time to see what goes on 'round here. What did she have to say about it?" Papa's forehead furrowed.

"I didn't ask. I told her it wasn't too late if she wanted out."

"What kind of an offer was that?" Papa sat up straight, setting one of his feet hard against the edge of the stool. "Of course it's too late. You two are young lovebirds out there around the trees. You love her, don't you?"

"Yes, but . . ."

"But nothing. What's she supposed to say to that? Don't go laying your insecurities at her feet. You're not giving her the credit she deserves. She's nothing like that gussied-up friend of hers. And if you can't see that, she's probably going to get tired of reassuring you all the time before she ever gets tired of the farm." Papa stopped talking and sat there, staring across the room.

Mark leaned against the wall and slid his hands into his pockets.

"What? Ya surprised I know a word like insecurities?"

Mark laughed. "No, but maybe that you knew I had some."

"Pshaw, everyone has 'em. But don't go letting 'em ruin a good thing."

A good thing. Mark thought of Angela before she left. She hadn't had an answer for him other than to ask if he thought she was so similar to Ashley. He banged the back of his head against the wall hard enough to rattle whatever was hanging on it.

"What about Nana?" Mark asked. "I know she loved the trees when I was boy, but how did she feel about them before you got married?"

Papa shifted his weight. He looked out the window, though there was nothing to see in the black of night except the rain running over the glass. "A remarkable woman, your nana. She grew up closer to downtown. Her father was a schoolteacher. She liked those books. But she and her father and her brother came out here in the summers for work." Papa's lips began to curl up in a playful smile. "I never did know if she fell in love with me that summer, or the trees."

"I remember her by the fire, reading. She told me more than once that a book and a tree could see her through the toughest of times," Mark remembered.

"Like I said—remarkable," Papa said. "Now that we're talking about it, I did make her a promise when we got married."

"You mean your vows?"

"No, a promise. I promised to love her. And even if she didn't love the land, I promised to love it so our children and our children's children would have a home and a place to grow and know what it meant to work hard and be loved." Papa met Mark's eyes for a moment. "That was enough for her."

"That ought to be enough for anybody," Mark said, still pondering it.

"Aw, just ask her, will ya?"

"You don't think it's too soon?"

"Too soon is better than too late."

The next day, Papa brought over the space heater Mark had ordered and set it beside the bed. Mark thanked him. Papa didn't leave but stood with his hands on his hips looking about the room.

"When you asked to trade places, I wasn't quite sure how it would go," Mark said.

"I know you thought I was crazy."

"No, but you and Mrs. Shaw hadn't even dated."

"Well, we will soon."

Mark suspected this, but he paused, waiting to see what else Papa would say about it. He moved the space heater to the other side of the room. Papa didn't say more.

"Thanks again for bringing this over."

"You sure you don't need an extra blanket? Nights will be getting colder."

Mark felt the quilt already on the bed. Thick and heavy. He'd be fine.

"And are you still planning to propose, then?" Mark asked.

"'Course I am. I wouldn't be helping you move for the fun of it. I don't rightly like the idea of moving myself. This here cabin has been good company."

"You know, Papa, I've been thinking. If Angela isn't fed up with my 'insecurities,' I'm planning on asking her soon. Tomorrow, actually. But I still don't know when we'll set a date."

"Now then, you need to defer to your bride-to-be when it comes to that."

"I'm trying to get the timing right," Mark said. "Do you have a place you want to go after . . . after Angela and I get . . .?"

"Go ahead. It helps to say it out loud—get married." Papa finished his sentence for him. "And, yes, I've thought about it."

"You know, I could see about adding another bedroom, another master. You were happy with our contractors." Mark paused here. Papa walked through the door of the bedroom. "That's sure to be too much money. How about you give me some notice when you think you might be needin' the place. Things have a way of workin' out."

Mark followed Papa out of the cabin. They stood on the steps outside the front door. "The wedding may not be for another year," Mark offered, trying to soften what felt more awkward than he'd imagined.

Papa eyed Mark. "Ask her. Then we'll talk."

Mark watched Papa walk along the path. He ran his hands through his hair and pulled at the back of his neck. He loved Angela more than he thought he could. And he was pretty sure Angela loved him. But did she love the farm? And would she still love it year after year? *Did* things have a way of working out? Was Papa right?

There was only one way to find out.

Mark called Angela on his way to the Historical Society to meet with Mrs. Simmons. A light rain covered the roads. He checked the edges of the horizon for a break in the clouds.

She answered but didn't sound too cheerful.

"Hey, I'm sorry about yesterday," he said.

"Go on," she said.

That wasn't the response he was hoping for.

"I didn't like the way things ended when you left. I've been worried about you and the farm. Most girls I've met haven't wanted anything to do with it." He started speaking too quickly, so he stopped to take a breath.

"I'm not most girls," Angela said with a little more emotion.

Sitting at a red light, Mark made another attempt. "I know. You're amazing. That's why I'm sorry. Maybe Ashley got to me. I know you didn't like Providence and you moved here and you're nothing like any of that. And I love you. And Papa said I was too full of insecurities, if you can believe that."

"You talked to Papa . . . about us?" Angela asked with the most emotion in her voice yet.

"You know Papa. He could tell something wasn't right with me."

"Did Papa say anything else I should know about?" she asked.

Mark wasn't sure, but her tone seemed to be shifting—maybe playful?

"He agreed I made a mess of things."

He also said to not waste time and just ask you to marry me.

"Well, I'm sorry too. I could have warned you about Ashley. She can be a bit much at first. I don't know why I got as upset as I did. When you said it wasn't too late . . . I don't know, it felt like you'd be fine if I left and didn't come back."

"That's not true. I would not be fine. If you're not still mad at me, can I take you to dinner tomorrow night?"

"Thursday?"

"I know, it's not like our usual Saturday-night date, but I thought it would be a good night for something special."

Something special like the autumnal equinox, which means we've officially known each other for four seasons.

"Okaaay?" Angela answered. "How special—what do you mean?"

Mark was almost to the Putnam Schoolhouse, where he was meeting Mrs. Simmons.

"How about I pick you up at five for an early dinner—the Millbury Steakhouse."

That way we can make it to the gazebo in town by six thirty—before sunset and before the Astronomy Club arrives.

"You don't have to do this because of Ashley. I'm fine."

"Has nothing to do with her. Promise."

"I'll be ready at five."

"Sounds good. Gotta go, but, hey, Angela? I love you," he said as directly as he knew how.

He heard Angela's nervous laugh through the phone.

"I love you too, Mark."

The white siding of the Putnam building took on a murky gray sheen in the rain. He parked and wanted to ignore the worry creeping in. It had been raining the last five or six days. Did he have any reason to believe it would stop tomorrow? Just because he's planned a date with Angela?

I should at least have a backup plan. Maybe come back to the farmhouse if the gazebo is too wet.

His insecurities returned at that thought. For as much as the farm would be the center of their lives, he wanted the proposal to take place somewhere else.

He saw Mrs. Simmons waiting by the window, one hand lifting the curtain, watching him approach. She quickly opened the door and ushered him inside.

"Here, wipe your shoes on this mat. This rain has everything covered in mud."

Mark did as instructed, more so because he felt like he'd walked back into his eighth-grade English class than because his shoes were muddy.

"Thanks for meeting with me today," he said quickly.

"Are you *the* Mark Shafer of the Shafer Tree Farm?"

"That's me."

"You were a student of mine, weren't you? I remember you, I do." She said this while looking about his head and shoulders. He stood about a foot taller than she did.

"I was afraid of that. Eighth grade might not have been my best year."

"Nonsense. You turned your papers in late, but do you know how thankful I was for your first essay? That "What did you do over the summer?" assignment was brutal. Every year I read twenty-five different descriptions of a trip to the beach, the lake, or an occasional trip down to Florida. But you—you wrote about your tree farm. And pruning the trees with your grandfather. And what it meant to you." She clapped her hands together and walked over to a desk at the back of the room. "An essay like that kept me going for another year."

Mark blushed, something he didn't often do. He could barely remember the essay, but he hoped her favorable memory would only help his cause.

"What brings you here today? You said something on the phone about the National Register," she asked, still cheerful.

"Right. I need to have the farm listed on the register, and from what I've read, the property needs to be recommended to the State Historical Society. Is that something you could help me with? Would you be willing to do that?" Mark still stood on the mat, wiping his feet a bit absentmindedly.

"Where did you read that? No, we—the State Historical Society—we do the recommending of your property to the National Register. Here, come sit down." She motioned to the chair across from her desk, then sat and began pulling out some file folders. She tapped on her keyboard while Mark took his seat.

"Is the farm in need of repair?" she asked curtly.

"Uh . . ." Mark had to think about it. "I'd say here and there. The roof will need attention soon. Some touch-up paint in places—"

"I mean do you plan to apply for a restoration grant? I'll tell you right now, those are hard to come by and you wouldn't be the first to go to all the trouble of getting listed only to find out the grants are scarce."

The exasperation in her voice reminded Mark of when she would lecture the class on a round of essays that were subpar.

"No, I wasn't even aware of grants. I mean, it's not money—the farm doesn't need restoring," he said.

Her eyes narrowed. The rain had picked up and was pounding against the frame walls.

"Advertising, then?" She sat back in her chair and crossed her arms.

Mark wasn't sure what she meant by this, either.

"No."

"You don't want to put up a billboard and maybe a sign or two to drum up more customers?" Her exasperation turned into contempt.

That's an idea, he thought, but he noted the look on her face.

"No, let me explain. I'm not sure if you've heard about the expansion of Route 146."

"Of course I've heard."

"They're planning a frontage road right through a section of the farm. And as much as I support the growth of Sutton, I don't think it should come at the cost of such a historically important piece of land as the tree farm."

He wasn't sure if he could make that claim about the farm being historically important, but the words came rolling out of his mouth that way. Maybe it had something to do with the English-class memories. He waited, listening to the rain and Mrs. Simmons tapping the desk with her pen.

"We certainly can't have that," she finally said. She moved to her computer and began clicking away. "You'll need my help. We can recommend your property to the National Register. It's the National Park Service in Washington, D.C. that makes the final review, and if they approve, *then* it will be listed by the Keeper of the National Register of Historic Places."

Mark smiled at the full name.

"Don't celebrate yet. It's not automatic. You can be turned down. But I'll do what I can. We may need a field visit. They have quarterly meetings and will probably want more information. It's a process." She looked at Mark, a bit more warmly now. As if they were on the same side.

"Thanks. Is there a fee? Do I pay you?" Mark asked as he stood.

"No fee. And seeing what a fine man you've become is enough." She peered at him over her glasses for a moment. "Any family yet?"

Mark grinned, not feeling older than the fourteen-year-old boy he was when she last saw him.

"Soon. Very soon," he answered, thinking of Angela and the gazebo and the ring.

CHAPTER 11

Angela called to Caroline, "Let's go. We've got to get you to school on time. Are you wearing the right shoes for PE?" Angela asked. "Don't you have that on Wednesdays?"

"Yes, Mom. I'm set. What are you doing today?" Caroline asked, slipping on her backpack.

Angela paused. *Working on a surprise for you.* "Taking care of some things at the farm," she answered. "Why do you ask?"

"Sometimes when you're going to the farm to see Mark, you're in a bigger hurry," Caroline said with a grin.

"Is that so? Well, today I happen to be helping Mrs. Shaw with some crafts."

"Which ones?"

"Uh, the reindeer made of out sticks," Angela said, not knowing if Mrs. Shaw would even be selling those this year.

"Yeah, those take a lot of work," Caroline nodded.

Thankfully, Caroline didn't ask any more questions as they navigated the school drop-off. It was hard to surprise a daughter who paid such close attention to details.

Thinking of surprises as she drove to the farm, she wondered again what Mark had added on. She had stopped asking months ago when he'd insisted it was a secret, but she did have a guess.

Less like a guess and more like a logical conclusion. Of course it was a new bedroom, probably a suite with a closet and bath. They'd talked about the space at the farmhouse and though it already had a master bedroom, it wasn't very large. She'd insisted that she didn't need a larger room, but Mark had started construction anyway.

Even Ashley assumed it was a bedroom. And thinking of that reminded Angela of her visit. The questions, the flirting. The *Tarzan* comment. And Mark's words, "*It's not too late.*"

She couldn't fault Mark for responding the way he did. She should have warned him. She could have prepared him. Maybe it would have gone better.

But he'd apologized, said he'd talked to Papa about what happened. About the two of them. It softened Angela's heart as she thought of it.

But she still wished he hadn't doubted her. Couldn't he tell she was different than Ashley?

Mrs. Shaw was a welcome sight. With a cheerful flip of her chin-length gray hair, she greeted Angela and ushered her to a side room in the craft barn where she'd set up painting stations.

"Miss Caroline doesn't suspect us, is that right?"

"As far as I can tell. She was satisfied when I told her you needed help with the stick-bundle reindeer. In fact, she nodded knowingly, like she understood how difficult those were to manage."

"Sounds like I better have one or two on display the next time she's here or she'll ask. Not much gets by her. A keen eye, that one."

Angela nodded as she took her seat at the table covered in butcher paper a bit distractedly as she thought of Mark proposing to Natalie, and the things he'd said to her after Ashley left.

"Was it something I said?" Mrs. Shaw asked.

"Hmm? What do you mean?"

"You look a bit distracted. Is Caroline okay?"

"Caroline. Yes, she's fine. Sorry, a little lost in thought," Angela replied, quickly picking up a paintbrush and choosing the garden shop from the collection of houses.

Mrs. Shaw had a church complete with a steeple in front of her and was lining up her paint colors. "How is your music going?" she asked while remaining focused on the paint.

"Good," Angela answered. "I sent some songs to the studio in Nashville, to that producer I met in the summer."

"The handsome one?"

"I never said that about him," Angela said, racing back through their conversations to be sure.

"You didn't have to." Mrs. Shaw smiled with raised eyebrows and then returned to focusing on painting the church. "I'm glad you're sending out your music. It means you're regaining your confidence. Gives you some joy, doesn't it?"

"Usually," Angela answered.

"But?"

"Mark and I were working on a song together." Angela checked Mrs. Shaw's face for judgment, though why, she wasn't sure. She'd never felt any from her before. "He was helping me with a song that needed a male voice."

"And you didn't like how it turned out? It can be tricky combining creative work with a relationship."

"No, that wasn't it. I loved his voice. It brought the song to life." Angela paused, not sure if she wanted to relive the episode.

"Something else?"

Angela mixed her paint colors rather vigorously.

"I still don't know how he managed it since he didn't own the house, but he proposed to Natalie. In the studio."

Angela continued painting the garden shop but glanced briefly at Mrs. Shaw, who had paused a moment with her paintbrush but didn't look up. Angela waited, painting the roof tiles with small strokes of black.

"He had no idea his future girlfriend would own that home," Mrs. Shaw stated.

"He could have told me," Angela said curtly.

"So the fact that he chose not to tell you until now is what bothers you?"

"I think so. He hadn't mentioned it before. Even though we've worked on music together plenty of times. We've made good memories there. At least I thought we did."

"You think those are ruined?" Mrs. Shaw put down her paintbrush, picked up a towel, and wiped her hands before she continued. "And what about Mark? Do you think he's happy about it? There isn't a thing the man can do about it now, is there." It wasn't a question.

Angela listened as she painted. "That's a good point. I took some time and drove out to the coast. It's me, not him. It brought up old emotions. Anyway, I thought I was over it, and then my friend Ashley visited the farm yesterday."

"A good friend?" Mrs. Shaw asked.

"I wouldn't say that." Angela stared at her garden shop. "We knew each other in high school. Her family was quite wealthy."

"Wasn't yours too?" Mrs. Shaw asked pointedly.

"Yes, but I don't know how to explain it."

Mrs. Shaw chuckled. "Her heart's set on that lifestyle and yours isn't."

"Yes. Thank you for recognizing that," Angela said, feeling validated. "If only Mark could have seen it that clearly."

"Oh, dear. What happened?"

"He thought I felt the same way about the farm as Ashley."

"That it wasn't nice enough?" Mrs. Shaw asked.

"It's fine now. He apologized, and so did I."

"Sounds like it's still bothering you. Give it time, then, if you're not ready to be gracious yet. But don't go punishin' a man you love for a simple misunderstanding. Don't be a punisher—that makes love an uphill trudge."

Gracious. After Mrs. Shaw stopped speaking, that word echoed loudest in Angela's mind. She liked it when she could be that way—gracious, generous, or at the very least *not petty*.

Don't be petty, she thought to herself and not for the first time.

Mrs. Shaw rummaged through her collection of paint bottles, looking for just the right shade of soft yellow so the windows could "glow with light."

"Seems to me some of the things that get us most upset open a door to us." She said this almost to herself, as if lost in thought. "Aha. Here it is."

"What do you mean, a door?" Angela asked.

"A new way of thinking. We can see things in a new way if we walk through the door. But if we're too angry, you know, the blind kind of angry, then we slam the door so quick and hard—and bam!—no light, no seeing things we could've seen." She held up the soft-yellow paint bottles and rocked them back and forth in her hands, like she was holding liquid light.

"I get it, but do you think that applies here? This is such a small thing. It's as if I know I'm overreacting again."

Mrs. Shaw interrupted oh so politely. "Walk through the door, my dear. If *you* had a broken engagement, one that brought you pain or humiliation—how eager would you be to share any of the details of it with Mark? And while you're walking through the door and looking at things in a new light, think of how worried Mark may be that you like this farm. Can't you understand why he might be sensitive about it?"

She had a point, one Angela couldn't refute mainly because she hadn't stopped long enough to think about how Mark felt about all of it. She let out another sigh.

"What is it, Angela? What's holding you back?" Mrs. Shaw asked, shifting in her chair to make eye contact with Angela.

Angela paused. It was no use to make something up or to brush off the question. This was Mrs. Shaw, after all. She finished painting the small evergreen wreath on the door of the shop.

"I don't want to make the same mistake. Or another completely new one, for that matter," Angela answered.

"Hmm. I see," Mrs. Shaw said and began painting again. Angela waited as several moments passed. Wasn't she going to say something? Offer advice? Anything?

The silence became almost too much. She stared at her half-painted garden shop and wanted to clean up and head home. It was as if Mrs. Shaw's lack of advice confirmed her greatest fear—that she could make another mistake, or that she already had.

"Are you leavin' it like that, then? Become unsure of yourself and your paintbrush and want to up and leave your shop undone?"

Angela hadn't heard this kind of impatient tone from Mrs. Shaw, at least not directed at her.

"I don't think I'm doing it justice. I probably should have added some snow patches on the roof," Angela said.

"That's it, then? One mistake and you walk away? Seems to me making no choice can be the mistake. Don't you owe it to Caroline to give your best?"

"Wait, are you talking about Mark or the garden shop?"

"Does it matter, dear?"

Angela sank back into her chair. She stared at the half-finished garden shop, and an unexpected thought sprung up. She imagined a garden next to the miniature building, full of flowers and fruits and vegetables. And a little man and woman cultivating it—maybe a husband and wife working side by side.

Gracious. New light. Give it my best.

"Speaking of doors and seeing things in a new light," Angela said, her thoughts turning to Mrs. Shaw, "have you ever thought about Papa, you know, maybe having him over for dinner sometime?"

"Not you too. Daft as a brush and not half as useful is all that is to me. Why does everyone assume that when there are two people over the age of sixty-five, they are automatically suited for marriage? When all they have in common is that they may be standing in the same room and not even near each other?" Mrs. Shaw's face reddened, and she stood and wiped her hands on her crafting apron. "Besides, I haven't got any use for marriage."

"I didn't say anything about that," Angela said. "Dinner, that's all."

"You didn't say it, but you don't know what you mean by dinner. Well, I do. You mean to say I should go chasin' Papa till he has pity on me and takes me on as his wife."

Angela had never heard her accent so thick or seen her mood change so quickly. What was that saying about protesting too loudly?

"I admit marriage did cross my mind, but only if you and Papa found something in each other you liked, something you could love."

"There, at least you admit it. We can be done with this nonsense, then?"

Angela rested her paintbrush. "Only if you tell me what you have against a little dinner."

"I don't object to dinner," Mrs. Shaw stated, returning to her calm and dignified way of speaking, "but I won't be the one cooking it. He can treat me if he's inclined."

Angela smiled slightly and returned to her painting.

"For the record, if Papa wanted to marry you, it wouldn't be for pity. I think he has his eye on you, and it's not pity on his face. Look at who Papa is and the way he takes care of the trees. He doesn't take the time to plant and nurture hundreds of trees out of pity. Whatever he does, he does for love."

Mrs. Shaw's face reflected the realization. Angela swelled with pleasure at being able to see something Mrs. Shaw couldn't. In her private reflecting, though, the words came back to her—about planting and nurturing. She gazed up through the side window of the barn at the ridge of trees greeting the horizon. Mark's hands had planted or pruned or protected most of the trees on that side of the farm.

It could only be for love.

"Hi, I . . . didn't know you were here," Mark said as he walked into the craft room of the barn but stopped short of approaching the table where Angela and Mrs. Shaw were painting.

His voice interrupted her thoughts of him. She looked up, and a smile crossed her face, but she let it drop quickly. She wasn't mad, but she didn't have that easy feeling. His smile fell too.

"Hello, Mark. It's good to see you today," Mrs. Shaw called out to him. "What brings you here?"

Angela watched his eyes dart to her before he answered.

"I, uh, I was looking for you, actually. I'm ordering some equipment—thought I better see if you needed anything for the barn."

Mrs. Shaw set down her paintbrush and wiped her hands on her apron. She pushed her chair away from the table. "I'd say I'm pretty well stocked. Papa's been seeing to that." She looked to Angela though she was still addressing Mark.

"Great. It'll be another day or two. If you think of anything, let me know," he said and paused.

Mrs. Shaw popped up out of her chair. "Let me check my book by the register. There may be something I need after all." On that last word, she looked to Angela again.

Though she knew exactly what Mrs. Shaw was up to, she wasn't happy about it. She and Mark were going to dinner tomorrow. They'd have alone time then. But Mrs. Shaw was already disappearing behind the door, and Mark still stood closer to the doorway than to her.

She put her paintbrush down and straightened up her workspace.

"We're about done," she said, keeping her voice neutral.

"Do you have a few minutes before you go? There's something I want to show you."

Angela turned enough to see his face. The question was still in his eyes. His heart-melting eyes.

"Sure, I just need to get home to Caroline soon."

"It won't take long," he said.

"Let me clean some of this up."

Without talking, he walked over and helped with the paint bottles and butcher paper. Mrs. Shaw returned and asked about the possibility of purchasing another dolly. She said the one they had was rather large and if she could have a smaller one, it would allow her to move boxes around without risking injury.

They headed back to the farmhouse and entered through the side door. Mark led them past the dining room and stopped at the painter's plastic draped strategically to obscure as much of the room as possible.

"I'm waiting for one last order—" He seemed to stop himself from elaborating. "I was going to wait until it was done, but I want to show you now."

Angela watched as he pulled some of the plastic down. She reached to take a sheet of it from his hands. It felt like they were unwrapping a present, and though she knew what it was, her stomach fluttered in excitement all the same.

Mark pulled away another sheet and took her hand to pull her through. She stood on a wide wooden floor that stretched to the wall where two large windows opened up to a stunning view of the trees.

Her breath caught, and she looked to Mark, a bit confused.

"Is this a . . . dining room?"

Mark only smiled. He walked her over to the adjoining room. She saw a control panel, chairs, a microphone—a music studio!

"Mark. This isn't a bedroom. It's not another master."

"You said you didn't need a larger one," he reminded her, checking her face. She heard a slight defensiveness in his tone.

"You're right, I don't. But all this time I thought . . . I thought you were building one anyway." She walked forward and let her fingers rest on the panel.

A recording room. A music room. She looked through a window to the room with the wooden floor. "And that is?" She turned back to ask Mark, but he was already at her side. He turned a few controls, adjusted the volume, and took her by the hand again.

In a blur of motion, they were in the middle of the floor, one of Angela's songs was playing, and they were dancing.

"How did you get my song? Was this always going to be a studio? . . . It had to be." She was answering her own questions. "You started this in the spring." She couldn't process it all quickly enough. As they turned, the trees kept coming into view and Mark still hadn't said anything. But he was smiling. She could almost hear his smile it was so broad.

"So to be clear, this is a dance floor?"

"You catch on quick," he said.

She loved it when they danced. Mark was happy, and she loved to be close to him when he was. Not to mention the feel of his arm draped across her back, her hands clasped around his neck.

Her song ended, and one of his started—the one she'd heard last week. She didn't welcome the thought of what had happened in her music studio, but a new realization settled over her. When Todd had left her, it felt like he had taken her dream of producing music with him. Here Mark was making that dream possible again. He had provided a place for them to work on their music together. A new place for the two of them.

"I'm in love. Can't get enough. Turning me upside down."

He pulled her close, clasping his hands at the small of her back, then leaned in and whispered, "I'm sorry, Angela. I never want to do anything to hurt you." He gently rested his head against hers.

She buried her head in his shoulder. She may or may not have been fighting back tears.

A few moments passed as they swayed to the music.

"Do you like it?" Mark asked quietly. "I want you to love it here. I want this to feel like home."

The only word that came to her mind was Mrs. Shaw's *gracious*. *How could she be anything but?*

"I *love* it Mark. And I love you," she said as she picked up her head and their lips met for a soft and earnest kiss.

CHAPTER 12

Mark never thought he'd be this excited for the first day of autumn. It wasn't the fall foliage. It wasn't the cooler temperatures. It was the start of the fourth season—the not-so-serious reason Angela had given for waiting to get married.

"You should know a man four seasons before you marry him," her mother had told her once. And somewhere along the way it had become a line in the sand. But it wasn't all bad. Mark noticed that Angela and her mother had been able to spend more time together. And it game him time to add on to the house.

But the calendar was on his side now, and the ring had been cleaned and appraised. They could have a little dinner, visit the gazebo, and come back to the farmhouse for some dancing. He would need to double-check with Papa to confirm he could spend some time at Mrs. Shaw's apartment.

He walked to the farmhouse and studied the cloud pattern in the sky.

At least it's not raining—at the moment.

He needed to order the sales tags for the upcoming season and check their quantities of herbicide—as well as pick up his new suit downtown. He was cutting it close having the alterations done and picking it up on the day of, but by the time he'd found a place to do it, there hadn't been much choice.

The phone rang. Mrs. Simmons wanted to talk to him right away.

"Good news. Are you ready for this?" She sounded out of breath. "A representative or two of the Massachusetts Historical Commission want to visit your farm today. Can you believe it? Neither can I. This is good news, Mark. They only meet quarterly, so I called them after you stopped by. It's a good thing I did."

"Today?" Mark asked, concerned his schedule would now be too tight.

"That's right. They wouldn't send someone out unless they thought the property deserved consideration. This means they will likely put it to a vote." Her voice reached a higher pitch as she finished, sounding like the property was as good as listed.

"Do you know what time?" He closed the equipment catalog on his desk, stood, and paced around the office. "What will I need to do?"

"The woman said three o'clock. That's okay with you, isn't it? I hope it is, since I already told her it was. Their meeting is next Friday, and they only had certain days for field visits. Are you getting a sense of what a miracle this is?"

"Yes, Mrs. Simmons, I can't thank you enough."

"Mark?" Her voice was now more intense. "Will you be ready to give her a tour? Do you have your criteria ready?"

"My criteria?" Mark stopped pacing and looked up at the trees through the office window.

"Please tell me you did your research. You do realize they will want to know your reasons." She sighed a heavy sigh. Mark could picture her in front of his English class again, like he'd gotten an assignment wrong—that he hadn't even turned in!

"Do you have something to write with? Between now and three o'clock you'll need to have an answer for these questions."

She spoke hurriedly. Mark scrawled the questions onto some note paper, asking her to repeat phrases only when absolutely necessary.

"How is the property associated with events of significant contribution to our history?"

"How is the property associated with the lives of significant persons in our past?"

Or was it "our significant past?"

Mark was trying to keep up. "Embodiment of distinctive characteristics," he wasn't sure he was spelling any of this correctly. "Yielding information significant in history."

At that, Mark felt the National Register possibility slip away. His voice had to have shown it as Mrs. Simmons began to be more encouraging.

"The farm only has to meet one of those criteria, Mark," she said, sounding pleased with herself. "Good luck, and tell me how it goes."

After the call, Mark sat back down at his desk and reread his notes.

This could take a while.

Deep into the history of Sutton and absorbed by the story of Rufus Putnam, a Revolutionary War soldier who helped defend Dorchester Heights and forced the British to abandon Boston, Mark was startled by the phone.

"Shafer Tree Farm, Mark speaking," he said with his eyes still on the computer.

"Checking in with you. I'll be in Sutton tomorrow. Have you had time to think about my offer?"

It took Mark a second—or less—to recognize John Jackson's voice. He was about to simply hang up, but something prevented him.

"John? Yeah, not sure what offer you're talking about, so no. I'm busy at the moment."

"I have an interested buyer. Not gonna lie—hard to come by with rumors flying about the expansion. And they aren't offering as much as you could have made last year. But given the circumstances, I can almost guarantee you'll make more than you would if you have to settle with the state."

Mark closed his eyes. He tried to breathe and count but didn't want to give John any more airtime that he already had.

He answered calmly. "The farm is not for sale, John. Not last year, not this year. And there won't be any settlement. I have good reason to believe the state will need to change its recommendation about the farm."

John scoffed. "Mark, do you hear yourself? The Department of Transportation gets whatever it wants around here, or haven't you noticed? I can save you a lot of grief. My buyer can meet—"

"Your buyer can go visit the Blackstone Street Bridge." Mark didn't raise his voice, but he could feel his temper rising. "The farm is being considered as a historic property, to be listed on the National Register."

Mark wished he'd hung up at the start. He didn't relish giving John any details, but he was determined to be done with his harassment.

"Are you kiddin' me? You think that's gonna happen?" John laughed—not a polite laugh. "Did you know Massachusetts has the most historic places listed on the National Register of any state in the country? Well, second to New York, but half their properties were probably bribes. Anyone can figure it out. They don't want any new listings from this state. There are over four thousand already. Ask me how I know. I'll tell you, selling real estate around this place, they're like landmines—everywhere you turn there's another place on the NR."

Mark listened, staring at his notes from Mrs. Simmons and the other notes he'd made from his research and doubted any of it would be enough.

"Unless you have, I don't know, Noah's ark in your backyard. I hate to be the one to tell you, but you don't have a chance."

Right. He loves being the one to tell me.

Mark glanced at the clock. It was approaching three.

"We'll see about that, John."

The rain had held off for most of the day, but the ground was saturated and water levels in the surrounding lakes were at record highs. At least the representatives of the Massachusetts Historical Commission didn't have to carry umbrellas.

Two men and a woman arrived in a Jeep. They all wore jeans, raincoats, and boots. Ready for the terrain. With John Jackson's words and laughter echoing in his ears, Mark greeted the group and invited them inside the farmhouse first. Maybe he could relax. If only John's call hadn't come before their inspection. If only it hadn't rattled his nerves.

The representatives were gracious and appeared genuinely interested in the farm. One of the men asked Mark how long he'd worked there, delighted to hear he was the descendant of the original settler. He saw the woman making notes. It didn't surprise him, but it didn't put him at ease either.

Once outside, he led them to the back lot of trees, avoiding the sales lot and Donna's barn. He wanted to downplay the commercial aspects of the farm. Based on Mrs. Simmons's questions, he thought that might count against him.

He spoke rapidly about tree varieties, planting schedules, and weather patterns. He detailed the types of herbicide they used, their procedures for controlling rodents, and even the best methods to ensure seedling survival.

When their eyes appeared glassed over, he began rambling about the several years of drought that had likely contributed to a large fire one year.

"My parents died in that fire," he said unintentionally.

At that, he stopped talking, stunned into silence at the thought that he had shared too much about the care of the trees and his personal life. They stood by the back of the farmhouse, having come full circle around the property.

He vaguely remembered the questions Mrs. Simmons had given him to research. He couldn't recall even one of them or an answer that might meet the listed criteria.

Finally, the woman slipped her pen into her raincoat pocket and said, "I'm sorry about your parents. That must have been very difficult for you. I'm sure it would please them very much to know you're taking such good care of the trees." She smiled and looked to the other gentlemen.

Mark exhaled. He hadn't intended to appeal to their sympathy. His nerves must have gotten the better of him.

"Can you tell me about your sales? You sell the trees for the holiday, right?" one of the men asked.

"Yes, we do. We have a small lot up front, to the side. We open after Thanksgiving and have a good number of families who return each year." Again, Mark wondered if any of this would hurt the application.

"Can you tell us about the cabin?" the other man asked.

Mark answered the few things that came to mind but regretted not finding out more before they came.

"And what about—was it your great-great-grandfather? Can you tell us more about him?"

Mark's mind went blank. He was failing not only the historical portion of the test but failing to answer the only question that mattered.

He saw Mrs. Shaw and Papa walk out of the side door of the farmhouse. Not wasting any time, he called to them and led the group to where Papa was.

"Papa, before you go, I'd like you to meet these visitors from the State Historical Commission." Mark handled the introductions and then repeated the last question he'd been unable to answer.

Knowing Papa, this could go either way.

"You mean Hans?" Papa clarified. "Sure, what do you want to know 'bout him?"

"Anything that might be significant relating to the history of the state or, if not, whatever you can tell us," the man said.

"Let's see, Hans Shafer was one of the first German settlers of Sutton. Wasn't easy, I suppose, with all the Englishmen already established around here. He had a kind of vision," Papa said.

Mark froze for a moment, hoping against hope he wasn't going to try to share keeper stories in place of historical facts. Then he remembered something Papa had told him. "He was one of the first commercial Christmas tree farmers, not only in Massachusetts but in the country. Right, Papa?"

"Yep, about 1920, '21. Took years before he made any profit. He was a man before his time."

The woman pulled out her pen and took more notes while the men exchanged satisfied looks. They talked with Papa about some of the development he had witnessed as a resident of Sutton for over seventy years.

They told Mark they would send the nomination form in and he would either get a letter from the National Park Service or a call from Mrs. Simmons. Then they excused themselves and were on their way.

Papa turned to Mark. "You mighta just saved the trees. And good thing. Don't you have a dinner to get to?"

Mark looked at his watch: 4:45 p.m.

CHAPTER 13

Angela parked her truck in the driveway of her home and tapped the steering wheel.
Thank you, thank you!

She headed inside, took a quick look in the mirror, and then checked the time. Forget redoing her hair. She'd barely have time to tame it. Apartment inspections in the rain had soaked it into a near-unmanageable mess. Add to that the fact that six days of rain and the resultant humidity had taken her naturally curly hair to new heights, very frizzy heights.

She heard her mother arrive and Caroline's chatter. She put on another layer of gloss and felt a twinge in her stomach. She refused to entertain the idea of Mark proposing.

I'm being ridiculous. This is just a date. So what if it's Thursday? And he asked to pick me up early. And said my little black dress would not be too formal. I have no reason to be nervous. Right?

With that unconvincing train of thought, she pulled out a different pair of heels. Slightly higher with straps. She stared at her feet in the mirror, one foot sporting a patent-leather bow and sturdy, low heel, and the other, the obvious winner, some eye-catching bling.

They hadn't done anything this formal since Valentine's Day and that was just for fun. She twisted her necklace around her neck, adjusting it needlessly. Saved from the endless, last-minute fussing by Caroline's voice calling from the front room.

"Mom? Isn't Mark supposed to be here now?"

Angela grabbed her wrap and purse and headed for the door. If only she could exit without passing the inspection crew.

No such luck.

"Ooooh, you're so pretty." Caroline jumped up from the sofa, staring at her mom in wide-eyed awe.

"I'm glad to see you haven't gotten rid of all your formal wear. I haven't even seen those shoes before. Are those Zanotti or Blahnik?"

"Please, Mom. These cost me $40, not $800."

"That might have been why I couldn't place them exactly. At least they are subtle."

Subtle?

In her younger years, her mother would say "If you can't wear designer, at least don't call attention to it with anything loud. No need to advertise the imitation."

"Somehow I don't think Mark will be worried about the shoes I'm wearing," Angela said, mostly to herself.

"Where are you off to, then?" Cathy asked.

"Dinner. An early dinner."

Though he did mention dancing.

The low heels were sounding much better.

"An early *formal* dinner," Cathy said as she smiled.

"I have no idea. It could be an anniversary of ours I haven't thought of yet."

"You didn't know Mark last September," Caroline piped up innocently.

Angela opened the refrigerator and pulled a few things from the back. She was still talking about what they could eat for dinner when Caroline opened the door and Mark walked in.

No, he didn't walk. He strode. He moved so smoothly and easily into the room and yet filled up the space with his suit-covered shoulders in such a way that Angela could not see anything else.

Or hear. Or think. Or do anything other than focus on her lungs to be sure she didn't stop breathing altogether. Not that she was thinking about any of this, but she was pretty sure she needed to keep breathing.

Mark smiled in her direction. She returned the smile but became awkwardly aware of the leftovers in her hand. Setting the containers down on the table, she greeted Mark.

"I'm ready. I was making sure Caroline and Mom would have plenty for dinner, but I'm ready to go."

"Go, then," Cathy said. "We'll be fine. Caroline has already taught me how to use your microwave. We might even try popcorn tonight."

Mark reached out his hand and Angela automatically reached out hers. She walked to his side as if they were the only two people in the room.

He kissed her cheek and said not too quietly, "You're beautiful."

What was going on here? Angela had gotten used to their Saturday-night dates. Casual, predictable, reliable. They had a good time. They were getting along fine. But this—what had changed? And it couldn't be just the suit, could it? For all her impatience with Ashley and the girl's obsession with men's fashion, she had to admit it had an effect.

"Is something wrong?" Mark asked.

"No. Not at all. I was um . . ." Angela looked down to Mark's feet and back up to his eyes. "I was admiring your suit. Have I ever seen you in this one?"

Mark laughed. "Ha. No, this is new for the occasion."

"And what occasion is that?" Cathy asked.

"Angela didn't tell you?"

All eyes were on a bewildered Angela. Mark held his lips together in a deliberate grin.

Finally he relented.

"It's the autumnal equinox," he said and whisked Angela out of the door before her mother or Caroline could ask any more questions. "And we've got reservations."

The restaurant had been quiet—not surprising for a weeknight. Mark dodged any questions about the equinox comment. He seemed happy but nervous, talkative but quick to change subjects.

Angela, though hungry from the longer-than-expected day she'd had, found she couldn't eat as much as she wanted. *So what if he's in a suit,* she told herself, *and acting funny. That doesn't mean anything. I have no reason to be nervous.*

His cell phone rang. She sipped her drink.

"We have to go," he said, waving to their waiter and standing. up. He reached for cash from his wallet.

"What? Now?"

Was this part of the plan for the night? Did he have a surprise party waiting for them or something?

But Mark was alarmed, frantic almost. "The farm. The rain. Brett said there might be overbank flooding from Lake Singletary."

"Isn't that ten miles away?"

"About that far. He said they don't know where the water's coming from, but a new channel of water has cut through the two-year-old's lot."

"Isn't that behind Donna's barn?"

"That's exactly where it is."

They both jumped out of Mark's truck as soon as he pulled up to the front door of the farmhouse. A quick glance at the ground and they could see that most of the water was rushing behind the house.

Mark pulled off his suit coat and threw it back into the truck. He did the same with his tie. He took the keys and put them in Angela's hand.

"Head inside. See if anyone else has been called. If you want to change into dry clothes"—he paused when they heard the sound of snapping branches—"there aren't any women's, but help yourself to anything dry that fits."

He bolted around the house. Angela stood for a moment, watching him go. Thunder cracked above her head. It shook her ribs and sent her running inside. She pulled off her strappy-heels, which were now useless, and made a beeline to Mark's bedroom only to see Papa's clothes in the drawer.

That's right, they traded places. Will I fit into any of this?

She opened and closed drawers and pulled open the closet doors. There, on the top of the closet shelf were some of Mark's clothes. She found a T-shirt and hoodie. Not that either would be helpful over the rain-soaked dress she had on. She pulled out the drawer with Papa's clothes one more time. There were several pairs of his jeans and one pair of carpenter-style Khaki's. She held them up to her waist and shook her head.

What difference does it make? He needs me out there.

She rolled the waist enough to tighten it and tucked the T-shirt in. Pulling the hoodie over her head, she could tell her hair was a lost cause. Without a ponytail holder, she wrestled it into a braided bun at the base of her neck.

Now dry, she ran to the phone at the front counter. Before she could call anyone, Brett came through the front door.

"Mark told me to call a few others," she said.

"Papa already called our seasonal team leader," Brett answered.

"Great, let's get out there," Angela said as she came out from around the counter.

Brett stared at her bare feet. "I don't think that's such a good idea."

"Blasted shoes. What size does Papa wear? Never mind, I'll figure something out."

"I'm bringing the truck around back with more sandbags," he said and left through the side door.

Angela dug into Mark's closet. She found a well-worn pair of boots, probably two sizes too big, but she stuffed one pair of socks in each of the toes, put another pair on, and laced up the boots.

She got to the side of Donna's barn a few minutes after Brett arrived. She didn't announce herself but grabbed a sandbag from the back of the truck Brett had driven to the side of the barn.

"Angela, is that you?" Mark called.

"Who did you think it was?"

"A much prettier Papa," Mark said without laughing. "You don't have to be out here."

"Whatever. You think I'm going to sit inside and sip hot cocoa?"

They moved in tandem, though Mark and Brett could lift two sandbags in the time it took Angela to lift one. Others filed in and without much discussion helped move the small mountain of sand to form a wall—protecting Donna's barn from the newly formed river beside it.

"Do you think the rain will let up?" Brett yelled to Mark.

"At this point, it doesn't much matter. I'm guessing Lake Singletary couldn't hold a week's worth of rain. I hope it's not the dam at the chasm. I don't know what else could cause this kind of water," Mark answered.

"Does that mean you don't *usually* have to worry about floods?" Angela asked.

"Papa said he hadn't seen it like this since '65," Brett said.

"Where is Papa, anyway?" Mark asked. They each paused and looked around. Somewhere in the frantic activity of the wall-building, they hadn't noticed he'd left.

Mark, Angela, and Brett approached Papa leaning on his shovel on top of the ridge behind the cabin. Together they surveyed the water. The volume had decreased but was flowing freely through the gulley that ran in between two lots of trees.

"Water found a way through here, but not before the swell took a piece of the cabin," Papa said.

Mark pivoted. Papa meant it literally. Several planks forming the wall on the west side were gone. It didn't look like much at a distance, but as Mark got closer he could see the path the water had taken, where it had retreated, and the debris it had left in its wake. As well as a tree that had fallen and crashed into the side of the cabin. As he stared at the hole left by the missing wood, he could see the obvious. An open door to as much water as could rush in.

"Papa, I'm sorry we didn't bring any sandbags over this way," Mark said.

"Those wouldn't have helped here. Water always wins. We couldn't have imagined it rising up that high, son." Papa took his shovel and scraped at the ground, enough to move some mud and sludge. "We've got some cleaning to do."

Mark motioned for Brett to help him with the tree.

"Let's get this out of the way."

Brett blinked at the tree at their feet. "Without a saw? This looks like it might have been fifteen or twenty feet tall."

Mark started to walk the length of it. "We don't have to move it very far. I'll sleep better knowing it's not part of the cabin. Let's see what we can do."

They each took hold of a side where the trunk had been stripped of some of its branches, then lifted and pulled it away from the cabin wall, once, and then twice.

On the third lift, as they walked it away a few more steps, the rocky and rain-soaked ground under Mark's feet gave way. His right leg buckled under him and he fell to the ground, his left leg extended under the tree.

"Mark!" Angela called.

"It's slipping!" Brett yelled, unable to hold the tree his own.

Mark felt a crushing weight against his leg before he saw it, before he could stop it. A searing pain shot up from his calf into his thigh. He instinctively pulled both legs away from the tree. His right foot gained traction, but his left leg was pinned.

Brett and Papa were already positioning themselves. "One, two, three."

They heaved the tree, and Mark jolted back. He jumped up on his right leg, putting a little weight on his left to test it.

"Is it broken?" Brett asked.

"I don't know," Mark said as he tested it again. "Ahhh. It's good. I'm fine."

"Let's get you inside," Papa said.

"What about the trees?" Mark asked.

"We'll worry about them tomorrow. Looks to me like we lost some fifth and sixth years. That will spell trouble for the next few years, but we won't know how much until we can take a closer look," Papa said.

"What about the seedlings—the ones we planted this April?"

"About those . . ." Papa said, setting his shovel against the cabin and walking back over the ridge. His hands rested on each hip, and his eyes lifted toward the darkening sky. "You may not believe this, but those trees hardly had a—"

Mark didn't wait for the bad news. He started limping toward the south section where they'd replanted, pain radiating from his left calf with every step. He was tired; they all were. But what did Papa mean? They couldn't be gone. Not those trees. Fire had claimed everything growing on that ground once and they'd waited until the year was right for new seedlings. Those trees had grown then, only for some vandals to cut them down in some senseless, destructive search for a treasure.

Mark had made sure the best seedlings were replanted there. He hadn't been at peace until they had taken root. They couldn't be gone.

They trudged through the receding water and the thick mud.

"You sure you ought to be walking on that leg of yours?" Papa asked.

"It's just bruised," he said, grimacing.

Any light from the sun behind the barricade of clouds was shrinking fast. But there was enough light to see his trees—his resolute seedlings, standing as though they didn't have a needle out of place. As though a storm had not been raging about their branches. Not even one of them downed.

"They're still standing," Brett said.

"I was trying to tell you that," Papa said.

"Incredible." Mark felt tears sting the corners of his eyes—not from the pain or the exhaustion but from the impossibly beautiful sight of those trees.

Once the others had left, Mark and Angela sat against the wall of the barn, the one opposite where the rushing water had threatened. A portable floodlight shone over their heads, illuminating a soft rain. They were protected from it by the eaves. Mark leaned his head back and closed his eyes. His arm rested on his right knee, a rain-soaked towel hanging from his hand. His suit pants were wet through and covered with mud.

Angela tucked her knees into her chest, resting her head on them, noticing Papa's pants for the first time since she put them on. She strained to hear the water. Had it slowed? She wasn't sure, but she could hear Mark's breathing. She took a measured breath of her own.

What time was it? She didn't look up. Or speak. The previous hours had been a blur of water and scramble and fury. One minute she and Mark were smiling over dinner, and the next they were wading through a river of tree branches and gravel. It could have been a thousand hours ago, but something nagged at the corner of her mind. Mark had been happy but nervous maybe? Just enough for Angela to feel uneasy. She exhaled. She couldn't be sure of anything at the moment. Her back ached; her legs too. The adrenaline rush was gone and all her energy and faculties with it.

Mark spoke with a strained but gentle voice. "You okay?"

Angela picked her head up enough to turn it, resting the side of her head on her knees. "Pretty great considering we saved Donna's barn. What about you?"

"This wasn't how I'd thought the night would go, you know?" She reached out and rubbed his arm. "I'm so sorry about your leg. Does it hurt?" she asked.

"It'll be fine." He clenched his jaw as he spoke.

"It hurts. I can tell," she said.

At this, he pushed his back against the wall and sat up straighter. He moved the towel from one hand to the other, and moved it over Angela's curved shoulders, then her arm.

She didn't move, only watched him with her eyes, sideways as they were.

He continued the motions of drying her back. Yes, she was drenched and the towel was soaked, but there was a careful, tender movement in his touch, one that surprised her. He took the towel and wrapped it around the ends of her long curly hair. Her braid had come undone amid the rain and chaos. Once, twice, he lifted it and held it in the towel. The towel couldn't absorb any more water, and they were covered in sand and grit, but his touch melted her, his love for her showing in his every motion. Such gentleness while he was sitting there in pain.

Their eyes met, and his hand rested on her back. A mix of warmth and grief filled her, and with no energy to resist her longing, she leaned into him.

"You must be freezing," he said, pulling her in, though his body was also drenched and not much warmer.

She nodded and moved her face to his. She closed her eyes as he put his lips to her forehead. She shivered involuntarily, and he pulled her tighter with both arms, adjusting his body to offer the most warmth possible. He kissed her forehead again, then her cheek, then her lips—lightly, slowly.

She sighed and he kissed her again. She reached around his neck and clasped her hands there. The damp coolness around them only accentuated the heat of their kiss, the heat rising inside her.

"Mark," she whispered, her eyes still closed. "What was it tonight, at dinner? Was something wrong?"

His tight embrace loosened, and he tilted his head away from her and exhaled.

"You want to know?"

He positioned himself at an angle so his back could be straight while one arm remained around her shoulder. "I was going to ask. I thought tonight, the autumnal equinox, would be a good night to."

"You aren't finishing your sentences."

"Propose. I was going to ask you, Angela, once and for all, to marry me. Not because it's been four seasons, not because Caroline chose a love-match tree, but because I love you. I love who you are and who I am when I'm with you. The more time we spend together, the more time I want to spend—loving you."

Angela couldn't fight the tears that welled up, spilled over, and streamed down her cheeks. She'd never felt so loved or cherished. She kissed him before he could say anything more.

He kissed her fiercely in return, holding her shoulders, moving his hands up to her face. He pulled back and met her searching eyes. He shifted his weight and knelt down on his right knee, twisting his left leg out of the way.

"Mark, your leg. What are you doing? Doesn't that hurt?"

"Will you, Angela? Will you marry me?"

Surprised, she gasped and locked eyes with him.

"Yes. Yes! Of course yes."

Mark stood, hopping slightly on his right leg, and pulled her up with him, then wrapped his arms around her waist and hugged her.

Angela reeled from the motion of it, her head woozy and heavy from the strain of the night. She leaned against his chest and let him squeeze her close. Why had she been so worried about the timing? She didn't want to live another day without Mark. A sob began in her chest, a sob of relief and exhaustion and joy.

"What is it?"

"I'm fine." She sobbed the words.

"Something's wrong." Mark pulled back to scan her face.

"I think I'm . . ."

"Tired. You must be. Here, we can sit back down." And they did.

"No, that isn't it, but thank you."

"Hungry? We can go inside and find something to eat."

"No, Mark, it's not that. I mean, yes, I'm hungry *and* tired. But if I didn't imagine what you just asked me, then I'm also engaged. And happy. Like, crazy happy. These are good tears," she said with another heave of her chest.

Mark didn't say anything for a minute. He just sat staring at her. "Maybe I ruined it, asking you here at a time like this."

"No," Angela said immediately. "Not ruined at all. I will

always be glad you asked me this very night, right after you singlehandedly saved the farm."

"I didn't do it by myself."

"Think of the story we can tell our children . . . our grandchildren," Angela said.

Mark smiled at those words.

"So what if we were drenched and exhausted? You were kneeling with a broken leg! Is it broken? Oh, I hope not," Angela said. "And so what if you didn't have the ring? We will never forget this night."

"The ring!" Mark began to dig in his pockets. "How did I forget it?" Any warmth of the moment gave way to a frantic chill. He searched his pockets over and over. "I put it in this pocket before I left the house. It's not here."

Angela replayed the rush to the farm, the swell of the river, the compromised bank, the mud and water and sand. Mark hadn't stopped moving, hadn't stopped working—he'd used every muscle, thrown his body into saving Donna's barn and the cabin. What was a little ring in the face of that frenzied work?

It was gone, that's what it was.

Angela reached for Mark's hands, taking them into her own, waiting for his eyes to meet hers.

Angela spoke quietly. "It's okay. Ring or no ring, I love you, and I will marry you."

CHAPTER 14

Neither Mark nor Papa got more than a few hours of sleep, he was sure of that. Yet here they were, walking early to survey the damage. A thick blanket of clouds still covered the sky, blocking any glow from the sunrise. Mark's eyes adjusted to the dark, and Papa's must have too. He was commenting on each section of trees they passed. Seemed the floodwaters had dislodged earth and rock and Papa's silence.

On any other day Mark would have had the chance to tell him about the good news—that he was engaged. But Papa was focused on the trees more intently than usual. He'd wait for a better time.

The dull ache in his left leg remained, and there was some swelling, but he was sure it wasn't broken. Bruised, maybe. The tree hadn't been that heavy.

"Whatcha gonna do about your leg?" Papa asked.

"Not much I can do. Let it be, I guess."

"Is it broken?"

"No, I'm walking on it. See?" Mark tried to walk unaffected.

"You a doctor now?"

Mark didn't reply. He didn't have anything against seeing a doctor. He just didn't have the time. By the look of things, there was more work to be done than he could have imagined.

"Look here," Papa said. "These two-year-olds had it rough. The water must have been almost as high as they are."

Sorrow welled up inside Mark. "Do we keep them? Or would it be better to clear the plot and see if we can get some mature seedlings next spring?" He weighed the options of letting the trees grow only for them to be ragged and unusable, or cutting them all down and starting over.

"Don't ask me," Papa said, staring at the debris of young branches below the trees. "Ask the trees."

Ask the trees?

"Why you starin' at me?"

"When you talk to the trees, do the trees talk back to you?" Mark asked.

"Why don't you plain out ask if it's time to send me to one of those homes for the senile? 'Course they don't talk back to me."

Papa didn't make eye contact but picked up a twisted branch at his foot and threw it off to the side of the path. This bewildered Mark. All this time it was as if Papa were leading up to this one skill—and now he was not only denying it, he was scoffing at it.

"Sorry, on all our walks it seemed . . ." Mark's voice trailed off.

"Look here." Papa stopped walking and faced the trees. "I said they don't talk back, but I still listen."

"So the trees *do* talk to you?"

Papa exhaled. "Talking isn't what I'd call it. That means they'd be speaking English, and it's not like that."

Mark waited.

"Every living thing has energy, has *an* energy. Trees—they live and breathe and . . . I think they feel. Maybe not in the way you and I do, but you've been in the room with a happy child, haven't you? No one needs to say a word, and I bet you can figure out right quick if that child is happy or sad. Am I right?" Papa asked.

Mark nodded, thinking of Caroline bubbling with enthusiasm around the trees.

"With practice, you can sense the energy that ebbs and flows and maybe the feelings. I kinda hoped that's what you've been doing with me. Maybe I should've been more specific."

Mark reviewed some of the walks he'd taken with Papa, trying to pinpoint if he'd felt anything like what Papa was describing. He hadn't thought much about feelings. Was that where the sadness was coming from? But was it the trees' or his own? Then there were the ideas he'd had—for the addition to the farmhouse and when he thought about selling again.

"Papa, have you ever gotten . . . never mind."

"Gotten what? C'mon now, you've already asked me if trees can talk."

"Have you ever had an idea, you know, gotten a specific idea from the trees, like instructions?" Mark waited for another scoff.

"Hmm. Now that's interesting. My father used to say . . ." Papa stopped talking and looked down at his hands, turned them over, then stared at the trees.

"Used to say what?" Mark asked.

"He said he got ideas from the trees all the time. Said 'bout the time he finished his walk, he'd have an idea in his mind that had never been there before." Papa stepped around a tiny tree, then crouched down to inspect it. "Can't say that's how it's been for me. I just feel what the trees feel. Not sure why, but for me, I have to get my own ideas." He sat up and studied Mark's face.

"Well?"

"Well, what?" Mark replied.

"What ideas have the trees been sharin' with you?"

Mark walked ahead of Papa a few steps, leaving a bit of space between them. He stared at the rain-soaked ground as he answered. "That addition to the back of the farmhouse. The entire picture of it came to my mind one morning."

"Yep. Sounds 'bout right."

"And one day, when I was thinking about the frontage road—I don't know, I felt like the trees told me they would stay, and I had this idea to research other properties. Saying it out loud makes it seem trivial. But is it even possible the trees could communicate that way?"

"Now don't go asking me to explain the mysteries of the universe. How am I supposed to know if it's the trees or something else? My father told me when I became the keeper, I'd have help from all of nature to do the work that needed to be done."

"All of nature?"

"And it could have something to do with the keeper's promise," Papa said quietly.

Mark had never heard of this. Not in all their walks or work or time spent on the farm.

"The what? You haven't said anything about this before."

Papa didn't respond.

Mark tightened up inside. After all these years, after all these months, there was still more that Papa hadn't confided in him. Didn't Papa trust him? Was it his memory? Had he simply forgotten what sounded like the most important piece to this whole puzzle?

"Papa, what is it? It sounds like something I should at least know about."

"Been wondering if you're ready, is all."

"Ready?" Mark tried to keep the alarm and disbelief out of his voice. "I thought I was ready last year!" He stopped and threw his hands in the air.

"If the trees are already giving you their ideas, I'd say it's time for secret number three. The promise."

They walked back to the farmhouse surveying the land and trees as they went, Mark and Papa in step with each other and quieter than they had been.

"Let's go inside and make it official."

Papa walked over to the shelves near the fireplace and took down the family Bible. He opened the front cover and then flipped through some pages. "Nope, not in there." He set it on the mantel and paced back and forth.

Mark's heart had been pounding in his chest, but now it beat even faster.

Papa stopped pacing. "Don't go worrying. It's around here somewhere."

"Around here somewhere?" Mark's mouth hung open. "You don't know where you put the tree-keeper's oath?"

"Not an oath, a promise. No raisin' the right hand, no swearing."

"But you lost it?"

"No, no. Now don't say that. It's been a few years, is all. It's short enough I might be able to remember it, but I don't want to get it wrong."

"Can I help you look for it?"

"It could be back in the cabin."

So off they went.

"The power is in the promise, Mark. Once you state your intention, once you make your commitment, nature takes notice.

THE TREE KEEPER'S PROMISE

There is trust, and the energy in the trees can combine and all that power will be directed to you," Papa said.

Mark watched his face. He thought he saw some sadness.

"Papa, is there something else going on here you're not telling me?"

Papa smiled wearily. "I'm telling you what you need to know."

"Yes, but why haven't you told me this sooner? Shouldn't I have made this promise last year? I thought that's when I became the keeper?"

"You did, and you have been," Papa said.

There wasn't much Mark could say. Papa could turn into a sealed vault without warning. Mark mulled over what he'd said already. And then it struck him.

"Once I make the promise, does that mean you won't be able to feel what the trees feel anymore?"

Papa smiled again, this time knowingly. "I thought you might figure it out. That is usually the way it works. It's not like flipping a switch, though. At least with my father it was gradual until . . ." He didn't finish.

"Until he couldn't sense anything?" Mark's heart sank. This couldn't be right. Why did it have to mean this for Papa?

"The trees only need one keeper at a time. That's how the energy works. And I'm sorry. You were ready last year, but I wasn't."

Mark's indignation softened as he thought about what this might do to Papa. "You'll be okay, right?" It felt like tears were stinging his eyes.

"'Course I'll be okay. What kind of a question is that? It's not like I'm dying. We've done enough talking. It's time to do this."

"Repeat after me. I—say your name, not mine," Papa advised, "promise to care for and keep the trees of the Shafer farm from all forms of danger and destruction with my body, heart, and mind."

Mark repeated each phrase as emphatically as Papa. His heart beat quicker in his chest, but as he finished, he felt mostly . . . the same.

"That's it?"

"Yep. It's not like a president's swearing in, but don't worry. The power is in the promise. You'll have what you need."

As Mark wondered if the promise lacked enough ceremony, Papa continued. "C'mon, we've got work to do."

He and Papa headed over to the sales lot. The water had cut a channel through it almost a foot deep, depositing most of the soil outside Donna's barn in the form of mud and debris. They would need to level out the ground in both areas as well as the ground by the trees near the cabin.

"See here. Can't have folks walking around this lot if it's full of hazards." Papa pointed to a cluster of barbed wire and nails. While the logs were heavy and the plant debris thick, they would have to use special care to comb the ground for any injurious matter.

Mark pulled his gloves tighter on his hands and began gathering the larger items. "I'll start a collection of this by our trash barrels. He glanced over at the spot behind and to the side of the farmhouse where they were kept. Gone. Of course.

Papa had noticed too. "Maybe we'll find 'em if we follow this channel."

They were stacking logs and piling up the debris when Papa asked about Angela.

"She isn't one to shy away from work, is she?" he said.

"Not at all, but even I was surprised," Mark said.

"There's no hiding what it means to take care of this land," Papa said as he stepped around a puddle. "Helps if she doesn't mind getting her hands dirty or, in this case, her feet wet."

"While we're talking about Angela, I have something to tell you," Mark said as he wiped his forehead with the back of his gloved hand. He couldn't hide his smile. "We're engaged."

"Now that's some good news. We need that around here." Papa straightened and stretched, swinging his arms around his back. He stared over the trees with a pleased expression on his face.

Mark looked around in Papa's direction. "Do the trees create love matches?" Mark asked.

"You know yourself these are miracle trees," Papa said slowly. "Isn't love the greatest miracle? What's the matter? You don't want to give 'em credit?"

"It's not that. It's just . . . they're trees. What could they possibly do to cause people to fall in love?"

"There you go again thinking about it all wrong." Papa sighed. He walked to another section of the sales lot and carried a cluster of broken branches and trash over to the debris piles.

"These trees bring people together. Like you and Angela, they brought you together, didn't they? But it's what you do with it that matters. Seems to me love is always a choice, always has been, always will be. Trees can't force anyone. They provide the love in the air," Papa added a wink, "but you've still got to do the work."

"Then what about having a wedding before Christmas?"

Papa grinned. "I can have a little fun every now and then."

They worked on the sales lot until Brett showed up with some of their seasonal employees. Mark and Papa left them to continue clearing the ground while they checked on the fencing on the north side of the farm. Papa suggested they pressure wash the barn after a few days when things had a chance to dry out. "No tellin' what came through in that water."

Mark said he'd already been on the phone with their equipment dealer. They would be delivering some fans and commercial dehumidifiers within a day or two. He would talk to him about a pressure washer, too.

They were walking on the higher ground of the farm. Water puddled in places from the rain. The torrent of water had not come up this high. As they moved through a row of three- and four-year-old trees, Mark thought of the promise he'd just made.

Care for and keep the trees . . . from all forms of danger . . . with my body, heart, and mind.

That was what he'd been doing ever since the day last year when he decided not to sell the farm. This wasn't new. But Papa did say he'd have help from all of nature.

He looked at the trees. What did that mean? He wasn't sure what he was waiting for exactly—maybe one of the trees to wave hello? Maybe the wind to swirl the leaves into a script formation with a message?

Anything to signal that something had changed.

Hadn't it?

They approached the section of the fence that had suffered the most damage. So many different thoughts had been filling his mind he almost forgot what they were doing there. Papa commented on lumber prices and if they should consider the PVC fencing he'd seen some of the other farms in the area use.

Mark was still staring at the trees.

Papa stopped and followed Mark's line of sight. "Remember, it's gradual."

"Thanks," Mark said. Not much felt different, and he'd already been wondering if Papa had made up the promise, but that wasn't like Papa.

They measured the ruined section of fence. It did make some sense, as long as they were replacing the damaged portion, to replace the fence with newer material. But the cost and time in addition to the other work they had from the flood—they agreed changing out the entire fence would need to wait.

They headed back to the sales lot to check in with Brett and walked along the eastern border, nearly making a full circle. Here they saw some of the most extensive damage. It seemed the surge of water that passed the cabin had continued on and torn through dozens and dozens of trees. Maybe hundreds.

Replant. They would replant. Yes, grief and a more physical pain than he wanted to admit were assaulting him, but stronger than these were his resolve and determination. Didn't matter how long it took. This was his land. These were his trees.

Mark felt a stir of wind, then a gust. He focused his attention on one tree in particular. He walked to it and reached for the trunk. A wave of melancholy hit him—not surprising, but somehow different than the sadness and grief he'd been feeling a minute ago. He stared at the tree for an explanation.

"What is it, Mark?" Papa asked.

Mark didn't take his eyes off the tree. "I'm not sure."

Papa continued walking. Mark stepped to the side of the tree to examine it. He was about to catch up with Papa and try to leave the feeling behind when he noticed the tiniest cluster of gray-green needles on one of the upper branches.

He stepped closer and scanned the rest of the tree but couldn't see any other discolored needles. Still, the faded green patch had that distinct gray hue.

Papa had returned. "Making a new friend?"

"Is this what I think it is?" Mark asked, motioning Papa toward the small cluster of needles on a partially obscured branch.

"I don't know. What do you think it is?" Papa answered.

"Pine wilt?"

Papa stared, then solemnly nodded his head. "It is. You sure caught it early. But it will still have to go."

"I'll let Brett know. Should we burn it or chip it?" Mark asked.

"Your choice. But how the dickens did you see that branch?"

THE TREE KEEPER'S PROMISE

Mark looked into Papa's face. The wind, the melancholy, the magnetic pull to that tree—was that all because of the promise?

"You don't have to answer that. Like I told you, the power is in the promise," Papa said. He was already walking ahead, and Mark ran to catch up but not to talk. His mind replayed what had happened—to memorize it, to maybe understand it.

"Papa, can I tell Angela about the promise?"

"You're gonna marry her, right?" Papa asked, a bit exasperated.

"Yes," Mark insisted.

"Then you better."

CHAPTER 15

Angela awoke Friday morning with flood-fighting weariness. She felt every muscle in her legs, including the ones she hadn't used since her step-aerobics craze. Caroline had come to check on her twice—once to ask if she could have the last of the Lucky Charms for breakfast, taking advantage of Angela's deep sleep, no doubt, and the second time to ask if Angela were sick and if she should call a doctor. Or maybe the friendly paramedic who took her to the hospital last year. Knowing Caroline, she could have that paramedic on the phone in minutes.

"I'm getting up right now," Angela said. As she sat up in bed, memories of the farm rushed back to her. The water and mud. The sandbags and the cabin. And Mark!

She instinctively reached for her hand and felt the bare space at the base of her finger. Mark's question. She wanted to hug him all over again.

Will you marry me?

She'd said yes. Of course she'd said yes.

A smile crossed her face.

"Are you ready?" Caroline came back to her room.

"Come sit on the end of my bed. I've got some news. You were asleep last night when I got home."

"You mean early this morning? Grandma told me it was 3:00 a.m.," Caroline said with a smile.

"Yes, earlier this morning. And she told you about the flood. But this is something that happened after." Angela paused, making sure she hadn't dreamt it. "Mark asked me to marry him last night."

"Serious? That's awesome!" Caroline jumped off the bed and then back on, closer to Angela, and gave her a big hug.

"I can tell you more about it on the way to school. I don't want you to be late," Angela said. She got up and dressed while Caroline ran back to the kitchen. She could hear her rinsing her cereal bowl and singing.

As they were headed out the door, Caroline stopped abruptly. "Do you know what this means? We'll be living at the farm for Christmas!"

"No, wait. We're barely engaged. We can't get married that soon," Angela said immediately.

"But Papa said."

"I know what he said, but Mark and I didn't even talk about a date. The farm was flooded. He—*we* have so much work to do," Angela said.

Caroline pulled on the straps of her backpack and climbed into the truck. As they drove to her school, she asked, "Where's your ring?"

Angela should have known better than to think Caroline wouldn't notice.

"Mark had it in his pocket at dinner but forgot about it when we rushed to the farm. We think it got lost in the water."

"You don't have it? Did you look everywhere?"

"Not everywhere. We were both exhausted."

By this time they were at the school and saying good-bye. As Caroline closed the truck door and Angela drove away, her cell phone rang.

Her mother.

"Good morning. Did Caroline make it to school on time?"

"I just dropped her off. Thanks for staying until I got back."

"I ought to have stayed till this morning. You must be exhausted," Cathy said.

"Yes, but I told you to go. You have a big day of shopping for your trip, don't you?"

"That's right, I do. It's so hard to predict what the weather will do when I'm there, I want to have enough warm clothes, but Nancy says—"

"Mark proposed last night." She said it quickly, as if she were ripping off a bandage. As interesting as her mother's vacation fashion woes sounded, she knew she wouldn't mind the interruption.

"Excuse me? Last night? And you're telling me now?"

"Mom, it's 8:45 in the morning. The only way you could have known sooner was if you'd been there!" she said as she pulled the truck into her driveway.

"You could have told me when you came in," she said flatly.

What difference did five hours make? For all of Angela's trying to help things stay good between them, it was moments like this where she questioned if it had been worth it.

"A minute ago you acknowledged how exhausted I must be. At 3:00 a.m. I wasn't in any condition to have this conversation," Angela said while internally scolding herself for sounding so defensive.

"This changes things. I can arrange to go shopping next week," her mother said.

"Why would you do that? What are you talking about?"

"We've got a wedding to plan! I'm thinking of two places. If I call right now, we may be able to get you booked before next year's holiday."

Angela let out a long, exasperated breath before speaking.

"Mom. No calls. No *places*. Mark and I don't have a date yet. I don't even have a ring," she said. "I'm headed over to the farm to help clean up."

There was silence between them.

"No ring?" Cathy finally asked.

"We think it was lost in the water. We're not sure," Angela said, kicking herself for even mentioning it. "Maybe it will turn up."

"But he did propose?"

"Yes! And this is where a normal mom might say something like 'Congratulations' or 'I'm happy for you,' not 'Why didn't you tell me five hours earlier?'" Angela got out of the truck and slammed her door, not caring if her mother heard it through the phone. She got as far as her porch and sat on her wicker chair.

"I'm sorry. Congratulations," Cathy said. "I got caught up in the excitement."

"Thank you," she said, relieved her mother was calmer.

"We could go look at a dress or two before I leave next week?"

Or not.

Without the strength to argue, Angela offered a simple "Maybe, if there's time."

She headed into her house to eat a little breakfast and planned to get to the farm to help clean up. As soon as she could get her legs to cooperate.

Her phone rang again. Not moving so quickly and convinced it was her mother calling with the guest list already compiled, she picked up on the last ring.

She heard a man's voice she didn't recognize.

"Angela, is that you? You there? I'll be in Sutton in a few hours. Are we still on for dinner?"

Her heart sank. "This must be . . . I'm sorry, what was it—John?"

"The one and only. What are the chances that we meet a week before I have some business in Sutton? You've got to admit that's pretty cool."

"Right. About that." Angela took a deep breath. *This should be easy*, she thought.

"There was a flood, and I'm exhausted. And, actually, I'm engaged," she said as she stared at her ring-less hand, shaking her head, wishing she'd said that first.

The line remained quiet for a moment.

"I gotta say, I wasn't expecting that. I tell you what. I'm still going to be in Sutton and there's a great steak house not too far away. Why don't you and your fiancé meet me there about six?"

"You really don't have to. With the flood, we have so much to clean up."

"A flood?" he said somewhat flatly. "That's too bad. I can't compete with that, now can I? Here's what I'll do. I've got some business over at the farm. I'll bring a little dinner to drop off to you. Does your fiancée work at the farm too?"

You could say that. "As a matter of fact, he does."

"Maybe I know this guy. I have some business with the farm."

If that were the case, Angela felt a wave of relief over not going to dinner with him simply to be polite. "What kind of business?" she asked.

"Do you know Mark Shafer, the owner? We had a buyer interested in the farm last year, but he passed on it. I don't usually do this, you know. When I go out of my way for someone and they pass up a great deal, I move on, but I can't help myself. Something about Mark—did you say you know him? Anyway, the farm won't be around much longer with MassDOT about to help themselves to most of the acreage. I'm going to do Mark a favor and get him more for the farm than he'll see from the state."

Shock seized Angela. She couldn't believe what she was hearing. "The farm won't be around much longer? Did I hear you right?" Angela stammered.

"I don't know MassDOT's timeline, but if your fiancée works there at the farm, he might want to start looking for another job. You know, I would."

"Another job," Angela repeated the words slowly but her mind was reeling, her heart racing. "So you'll be at the farm in a few hours?"

"Yeah, I'll bring something, maybe pizza for everyone. Courtesy of John Jackson Development. Least I can do. And you can introduce me to your fiancée. See you about six. Gotta go."

"Okay." *Not okay. What am I saying?*

"And, Angela," he said pointedly, "congratulations on your engagement. Whoever it is, he's a lucky guy."

With that, he hung up.

He's lucky, all right.

The fatigue had left her muscles, which were now powered by pure outrage. How could he? How *dare* he? Sell the farm?

She replayed John's words. She analyzed them for anything she could have misunderstood. No matter which way she replayed the conversation—he had been clear about one thing: the farm wouldn't be around much longer.

And Mark hadn't said a thing. Not one word.

When exactly was he planning on telling her? After he proposed? After they married?

On the way to the farm, Angela tried to cool her boiling emotions. *There has to be more to the story,* she told herself. *Maybe this John has his facts confused. Maybe he's thinking of another farm.*

Unlikely, and she knew it. The pit in her stomach grew larger.

THE TREE KEEPER'S PROMISE

When she arrived and parked, she looked at the trees from the east to the ones that had been battered by the floodwaters. John's words echoed in her mind. "The farm won't be around much longer."

He has to be wrong.

She marched to the front door and found no one inside. Of course they'd be working, cleaning up after last night.

Brett walked up on the porch at the same time that she was coming out of the house.

"Where's Mark?" she asked without a proper greeting.

"Not here. You okay?" Brett asked.

"No. Where is he?"

"After he got back from the doctor, he headed over to Bill's Lumber Yard. The shed behind the cabin is mostly gone."

She thought about what had happened there. *That's right. His leg.*

"Do you know if his leg is broken?" she asked, hoping for Mark's sake it wasn't.

"I'm not sure, he was walking better on it this morning."

"When do you think he'll be back?"

"Don't know, but can I help you with anything?" Brett asked.

She eyed him and took a deep breath. She wanted to ask if Mark had told him. Had Mark told everyone but her? But something calmed her, maybe being at the farm and feeling like it was so . . . so permanent, that whatever John Jackson was talking about couldn't possibly be true.

"Sorry Brett," she said. "You know what, I'll talk to him when he gets back. I'm sure it will all be fine." Her voice rose on the last word, still trying to convince herself. "What can I help with while I'm here?"

"I'm sure Mrs. Shaw would love your help in the craft barn."

"Of course."

It wasn't any easier talking to Mrs. Shaw than it had been talking to Brett. But being with her helped Angela feel hopeful. There had to be a logical explanation. *Right?*

They worked side by side on the shelves at the back corner of the barn where the water had done the most damage. Mrs. Shaw had strung a clothesline across the barn with all sizes of clothespins, a rather ingenious way to air out all the merchandise. The two of them hung the soggy crafts on the line, at least those that were salvageable.

Mrs. Shaw wasn't so talkative, focused as she was. She repeated several times how much worse it could have been, what a miracle it was that Mark had built that addition. The flow of water had been diverted mostly around the barn.

The addition. Angela paused at the mention of it. He built a music studio and a dance floor for her, for them. Why would he have added any rooms at all to a farmhouse he was planning to sell? Something wasn't adding up. *Maybe John was wrong.*

Useless. It was useless to figure anything out without talking to Mark. That's what she wanted to do, but she couldn't let it go.

"Mrs. Shaw, can I ask you a hypothetical question?"

"If you have to. I'll have to give you a hypothetical answer," she said with that British cheekiness of hers.

"What do you do if you find out someone close to you has been keeping something from you?"

"Oh, dear, that's not hypothetical, it's hazardous," she said as she clipped some felt wreaths to the line. She brushed her hands together and then on her apron. "I don't know that I want to venture into those waters—pardon my pun."

"Sorry. I don't mean to make you uncomfortable. But there's something I don't know and want to know. Wouldn't you . . . want to know?" She paused. "Hypothetically speaking."

"Depends on who you are. Now, my Auntie Joan, she wanted nothing to do with secrets. If someone was keeping something to themselves, she'd say 'Probably a good reason for it.' She would also say, 'Secrets are usually problems, and I got enough of my own. Don't need anybody else's.' Depends on who you are." She gave Angela a sideways look.

"But what if their secret could hurt a lot of people?"

"See, now, that's what I meant by hazardous. I don't want to be awake tonight wondering what you're talking about. If you think anyone is in danger, you ought to talk to the person. Plain and simple."

Angela's stomach churned, and her mouth went dry. That's what she wanted to do—talk to Mark. She was trying not to assume the worst. She wanted to give him the benefit of the doubt. Had Todd ruined her ability to trust?

Mark burst through the door.

"Hi there, ladies! Looks like you've got things under control in here."

Angela looked up to see a tired Mark, his hat on backward, his jacket wet. But he had a big smile across his face. He walked straight toward her with the slightest limp, setting down some tools on a shelf so both his arms were free. Before Angela could even brace herself, Mark put both arms around her and lifted her up, then spun her a half turn before he put her back down.

"Has Angela been telling you what happened after the flood?"

Angela laughed at the unexpected embrace and then realized why Mark was so happy, where all his energy was coming from.

"After the flood? No she hasn't," Mrs. Shaw answered, looking to their faces for answers.

Angela hadn't been sure if they were sharing the news yet, and she obviously had other things on her mind.

Mark looked to Angela as if to ask, "Why not?"

With both feet back on the floor, Angela regained her balance and quickly thought of a response. "I was waiting for you." *Which was somewhat true . . .*

"Shared news?" Mrs. Shaw asked. "Go on, do tell."

Angela looked to Mark, and he nodded, though it didn't look like he could wait one more minute.

"We're engaged," she said.

"Now that's news! It took a flood, did it?"

Mark spoke up. "I'd taken her to dinner and was going to ask her at the gazebo in town—and then we got the call from Papa."

"I didn't know that," Angela said. She'd had no idea he'd planned it at a romantic place.

He still had his arm around her, and she liked the security of it. She didn't want anything to get in the way of that.

"It was supposed to be a surprise," Mark said.

"Congratulations, you two." When Mrs. Shaw gave Angela the funniest look, Angela suddenly realized what they'd been talking about before Mark arrived.

As she dried her hands on her jeans and took Mark's hand, she asked Mrs. Shaw if she could manage on her own for a bit. She and Mark needed to "catch up."

Angela asked Mark about his leg. The doctor said it wasn't broken, yet he walked like it could be.

"Mild ligament sprain," he said. "Three or four weeks and it'll be as good as new."

"Is it bothering you, though?" she asked.

"Only if it stops me from dancing with you on our new floor," he said, smiling.

Mark, it seemed, was full of a happy energy, while Angela was quietly trying to decide how to ask him about what John Jackson had told her. And why would he build a studio with a dance floor in a house that he wasn't going to keep? As they rounded the side of the house to the front porch, she decided she couldn't wait for the right words.

"Why are you selling the farm?"

He stopped short, turning to her in shock. "What are you talking about?"

"I heard about the Department of Transportation—the man I met, the one who offered to help me when the truck wouldn't start."

"The guy in Fall River?" Mark asked.

"He called me and told me about MassDOT and a deal. That you're selling the farm." Angela's voice shook, though she tried to slow down and steady it.

"What do you mean he called you? Deal? What deal?"

She paused long enough to look directly at him, the indignation rising inside her. He looked sincere, but then again, he *always* looked sincere. Would he own up to a secret like this?

"Don't do this, Mark."

"Do what?" He threw is hands up and gestured to the house.

"It's bad enough you didn't tell me in the first place. But to stand here and deny it makes it so much worse. I need to be able to trust you." She could feel her throat tighten and the tears well up. She did *so* not want to cry. She turned her back on him and took a few steps as if she were headed back to the barn, but something felt wrong. She didn't want to be walking away from him or turning her back on him.

What if he were telling the truth?

"You're *not* selling the farm?" she asked.

"No! And I'm not denying anything. There is no deal."

Relief washed over her. This was the Mark she knew. He

caught up to her and reached out for her arm. "What exactly did this guy say?"

"Something about MassDOT and the farm not being around much longer. Do you have any idea what he's talking about?" she asked.

"I was going to tell you," he said, scratching the side of his head. "It's the expansion of 146 and a frontage road. It had gotten so busy with the farm. And I was planning our date."

"So they do want the land? They are going to put in a new road?" she asked, more alarmed than before.

"Yes, but no," he said, reaching for her hand. "I've been working on it. I've talked to a lawyer, and Papa and I met with some people from the historical commission. We hope we've found a way to prevent them from using the land. I was waiting to tell you when I was sure it was good news," he said. She could see the weariness in his face, the pressure he'd been under.

"I knew there had to be an explanation. I'm sorry," she said. She moved closer to him for a hug, which he quickly gave her. "You know you can tell me any news, good or bad, right?"

"You're right. I could have told you sooner," he said.

"So, then, what business does he have here?" she asked after a moment.

"He's coming here? Who is this guy?" Mark asked.

"Hi, you two. I came as soon as I heard."

Angela heard the voice. "Ashley, what are you doing here?"

CHAPTER 16

None of what Angela had said to him made much sense. If he wasn't selling the farm, how could she have heard from *anyone* that he was? They hadn't even been engaged twenty-four hours and the farm was in chaos, and now some rumor had gotten started about the sale of it. But Papa had warned him about not telling Angela about MassDOT's plans. He should have listened. It would have prevented some of this confusion.

But what could Ashley possibly want on a day like today? He glanced at her feet. At least she had enough sense to wear boots without heels this time.

She was speaking to Angela. "I heard what happened. I was at the manager's office this morning. I met your friend, that sweet grandma. You didn't tell me she works here at the farm too. I'm getting the idea that this is *the* coolest place in Sutton."

She made eye contact with Mark on that word. He wasn't up for this today. He looked toward Angela, who didn't look like she was up for it either.

"Of course *we* think so," Mark said, though it was hard for him to make small talk.

"It was good of you to come," Angela said. "We can use every extra pair of helping hands for the cleanup effort."

Ashley's eyes widened, and she even stepped away from Angela, just a half step, but it was clear she was uncomfortable. "Cleanup . . . I didn't think of that. And, darn, I can't stay. My dog has a grooming appointment."

Mark wanted to excuse himself. Before he could, Ashley turned and asked him for his help getting some things from her car. Angela offered to help too, and in a way that gave him the impression she didn't want them to have any alone time. Which was fine by Mark.

"As soon as your friend told me about the rain and the flood, I thought, *What would they need with all that water?* And the only thing I could think of was the day our hot tub had a leak and we didn't know it. We could *not* figure out where all the water was coming from."

Mark glanced to Angela, who was also trying to suppress a reaction.

"The way the deck was designed—badly designed—we had water leaking right into the house! Anyway," she continued talking even as she was leaning into her car to retrieve what she'd brought, "I knew you'd need as many of these as you could get."

She held up a stack of towels.

Neither he nor Angela spoke for moment. Ashley looked back and forth between them, waiting for a response, an acknowledgment, anything.

"Here, I can take those. Thank you. This was so thoughtful of you," Mark said. "You didn't have to drive all this way."

After Mark took the stack from her hand, she turned and retrieved another pile from her car and handed them to Angela.

"More towels. Wow, you shouldn't have. This is generous of you," Angela said.

"I already feel so much better knowing you can stay dry out here," Ashley said, beaming at the two of them. As she announced it was time for her to go, a black Hummer drove into the parking lot and pulled up right next to Ashley's Mazda.

Before the door opened and the driver jumped out, it all clicked in Mark's mind. The man who had *helped* Angela, the man who called her and lied about a deal, was—

"John. John Jackson, good to meet you," he said as he shook Ashley's hand—who appeared to be fascinated by his name alone. "Doing some business here. I don't believe we've met."

Angela made a start at introductions, but Ashley carried on as if she were the only one there. "You can call me Ashley. Nice to meet you." She flipped her hair. She seemed to do that a lot. "Shame. I was just leaving," she said.

"There's no business happening here," Mark said directly to John, not caring at all if he interrupted a *moment*.

"Are you sure you don't want to stay for a bite to eat?" John produced three pizza boxes.

"There's no dinner happening here, either," Mark said as indignantly as he could while holding a wobbly stack of towels. He trained his eyes on John. Angela and Ashley were speaking, but he seemed to have tuned it out.

"You couldn't use some pizza? I heard you had a rough night. Tough break with the rain and the banks of Singletary giving out. I thought we could go over some of the specifics about the farm. According to MassDOT—"

Mark turned to Angela. He gave her his stack of towels to hold with her other hand. Not an easy task, but she managed it. He then walked over to John, took the pizzas, and gave them directly to Ashley.

"There. Ashley came all this way to help us. She'll enjoy these."

"Um, I have this gluten—" Ashley began. Mark gave her a quick look, and she backpedaled. "I can . . . sure. Thank you." She put them in her car and hopped in.

"You can leave now too," he said to John.

"What about my offer?" John asked.

"Not interested." Mark turned his back on him and walked to where Angela stood.

"You don't want to make another mistake, do you? I'm your last hope. If you pass up my offer, you're on your own, and I don't think you're any match for the state."

"*You* are not my hope, last or otherwise. And I'm not making a mistake. Go ahead and leave. We've got a lot of work to do here. Real work."

Mark and Angela took the oversized, designer towels to the farmhouse.

"She meant well," Angela said.

Mark didn't reply. He might have contained his anger while he'd talked to John Jackson, but it was still threatening at the surface.

"I'm sorry about earlier. About not talking to you, not asking you before I jumped to conclusions," Angela said.

At that, Mark reached over for another hug. He didn't want to take out any of his frustration on her. "How did you say you ran into him?"

"I was in Fall River," Angela said hesitatingly, pulling back from the hug.

"And why did you go there again?" Mark asked.

"I tried to find Dona Florinda—she used to live there with her cousin."

"You drove out there on a whim, no checking on the address first?"

"I didn't know I'd be out that way. I actually just went for a drive. I needed some space to think." Angela's voice trailed off.

"About us? You needed to think about us?"

"Yes," she admitted. "But mostly about me. I had to sort some things out."

"So where did you go?"

"The beach. Same one I used to go to with my friends."

They walked into the kitchen at Mark's lead. He poured a protein shake and offered Angela some.

"You know, you didn't have to go that far. Sutton might not have the ocean, but there are some places definitely removed from people." He was thinking of Purgatory Chasm. His father had taken him there in the summers. He'd gone exploring there with his high school friends. And a few times when he needed a place to think outside the farm. It had been years since he'd been there, though.

"How about in a few days, when we need a break from the mud around here, I pick you up and take you to a place I think you'll like?"

"Have I been there before?"

"Maybe. It will be a good place for us to talk. There's something I want to tell you."

CHAPTER 17

It was hard to believe the flood at the farm had only been a week ago. Angela had spent every moment that she wasn't helping Ashley with the management office over at the farm helping with the cleanup effort. Mostly she helped Mrs. Shaw, who insisted on removing every last craft and treating the barn with undiluted vinegar, claiming it would prevent mold. And though only some of the inventory in boxes had water damage, Mrs. Shaw wanted to inspect each and every craft item.

They stopped for lunch, and Mrs. Shaw dismissed Angela.

"Go on. You've got to go. You've been here too long as it is."

"I still have two hours before I need to be at my mom's. Her plane doesn't even leave until six tonight."

"Just so, she may need your help with her luggage, or she may want your company before she's off to the other side of the Atlantic. You've given me more help than I knew I needed. Now go."

Angela gathered her sweater and purse. They had worked all week, but Angela hadn't had a chance to ask about Papa.

"Before I go, is there any news you have to share?"

Mrs. Shaw seemed a little too interested in some knitted stockings. "Drive safe," she said as if she hadn't heard her.

"That confirms it, then." Angela smiled knowingly. "You aren't going to elope are you?"

With that, the woman's eyes widened and she huffed over to another table where they had laid out gingerbread ornaments. "We were planning to catch up with you and Mark tonight. I wanted to be done with all these bits n' bobs first." She put down the ornaments with an exaggerated sigh. "No sense in waiting longer, is there?" she said. "Would you be mad to know we've been engaged for some time now? Alberto thought it best to wait until you and Mark made it official."

Alberto? Angela hadn't heard anyone call him by his given name—ever. With the way they'd both been acting, this confirmed what she'd suspected.

"As for eloping, I told him we didn't need a big or fancy ceremony, but it must be in the church."

This was news to Angela. Not that they had talked about it, but she didn't know Mrs. Shaw was particular on this point.

"The First Congregational Church—you have seen it, haven't you? An October wedding on my mother's birthday, Angela. It will be lovely, just lovely."

"And her birthday is when?"

"The twenty-second. A bit soon, but why should we wait? We're not getting any younger." She giggled a bit to herself.

Angela couldn't help but feel her delight, but given their friendship, she had to ask. "You know, once upon a time you said you didn't have much use for marriage. What changed your mind?"

"Not what. Who. Alberto, that's who." Her face changed from giddy to reverent and then softened into another smile. "I was only saying the same things the uninvolved say about happy couples. You didn't believe my blathering, did you?"

"Hmm. I see. Maybe a little. You can be convincing."

"Now, before you go. I've got something for you." She returned from the back room with a large box she handed Angela.

"It's heavy. What is this for?"

"Have you given Caroline the garden shop?"

"Not yet. I thought I'd wait."

"That box has the church," she said. "And the other pieces I have. Most are painted. There are two more. Maybe you'll have time to finish them."

"We said we were going to add to the village each year!"

"I know, but I couldn't help myself. I fell in love with the bakery and then had to do the blacksmith's house. And the toy shop."

"Where will we put all of these?" Angela asked. "There are too many. You can't give us all of them."

"Nonsense. I can, and I have. Now, if you don't have paints at home, bring Caroline here and she can paint the rest."

"Thank you! I'll find a way to repay you," Angela said.

"Then it wouldn't be a gift," she said. "Alberto and I will still come by tonight—after dinner."

Caroline had been quiet for most of the ride back from the airport. Angela attributed this to missing playtime with Gary's dog, though he'd reassured her he'd like to bring Bones out to the farm one weekend.

"She isn't coming back until November," Caroline said as they neared their house on Hickory Avenue.

"Hopefully she'll be back for Thanksgiving. But, remember, this is something she's wanted to do most of her life," Angela explained. "She'll probably find reasons to extend her stay."

"What did she mean when she said, 'We'll do something about the ring when I get back'?" Caroline asked.

"She means my engagement ring. She can't believe I told Mark I don't need one, at least not right away."

"Has he looked for it in the last place he saw it, like you tell me to do?"

"Yes, he has."

"Hmm. Do you think Grandma will buy you one, like she did with the house?"

"I hope not. She's done enough. Besides, that's for Mark and me to work out."

It was quiet for another moment, and Caroline had not perked up.

"I was going to wait, but when we get home I have a surprise."

"For me? What is it?"

"I thought we'd start our own Christmas village this year."

"Like one we can put under the tree?"

When they got in the door, it was the first thing Caroline

wanted to see. Angela gave her the garden shop, not disclosing that the rest of the village was in the box.

Caroline took it reverently. "I love it! Wait, did you paint this?"

"I did," Angela said, a bit proud of herself. And relieved to see a spark of joy return to her daughter's eyes.

"It's beautiful. I love it," she said. "And you know what else? I have a feeling Mark is going to find your ring," Caroline said firmly.

Where did that come from?

"Is that so? Sorry, but I think it's gone with the floodwaters."

"Don't be so sure. We're putting up a Shafer tree for Christmas. You never know what can happen."

Mark and Angela finished the dinner dishes together after Caroline had gone to sleep. She told him he didn't need to help. She knew he was exhausted from the work at the farm, which was why she had insisted he come to dinner at her house. She hoped he could relax. But standing next to her and putting the dishes into the dishwasher allowed him to be that much closer to her, he'd said.

They heard a pounding on the front door. She checked the wall clock in the hallway: 9:35 p.m. Not terribly late. She looked down the hall to Caroline's room and saw that her light was still off. Mark went over to answer the door.

"Papa?" he asked. "Mrs. Shaw? Come in, you two."

"We won't keep you long. Dorothy said tonight was a good night to stop by," Papa said with a smile.

Angela looked first at Papa, then at Mrs. Shaw. *Dorothy?* She knew that was her name, but this was the first she'd heard Papa, or anyone, use it.

It occurred to her they all called her Mrs. Shaw. Once she married Papa, that name wouldn't exactly fit.

"Maybe it is too late. Sorry dear."

"No, not too late at all, Mrs. Sh—um, *Dorothy*." This would take some getting used to.

"Have a seat."

Papa and Dorothy sat on one end of the sofa while Mark sat on the other. Angela sat in the chair.

"Is everything okay?" Mark asked. Papa's face registered a smile.

"Better than ever," Papa answered quickly, winking at Mrs. Shaw—*Dorothy*.

"Did your mother make her flight?" she asked.

"Yes, she's off," Angela replied.

Papa and Dorothy held hands. Angela could see Mark shift.

"How about something to drink?" She jumped out of her chair to the kitchen. The glasses clanged onto the counter.

"I won't be needin' a drink," Papa said.

"Some water is all I need, dear."

As Angela returned to her chair, she saw that Papa had stopped holding Dorothy's hand, which might have helped Mark's nerves. Only now, Papa was draping his arm across her shoulders as he reclined against the sofa.

"We thought it best to tell you. We're engaged," Dorothy said.

"Yes, we are. Dorothy and I, we're goin' to tie the knot. I'll be the luckiest man in Sutton. Wouldn't you say?" He looked at Dorothy with a big grin.

"Yes, you will." She patted him on the knee, and Angela checked Mark for reaction. He'd been quiet so far.

"Congratulations, Papa, Mrs. Shaw," Mark finally said.

"Thank you, Mark. I know it may take some getting used to, but call me Dorothy. Please."

This request made Angela realize Dorothy would soon have a new name: *Mrs. Shafer*. That thought somehow provoked what? Jealousy?

Angela studied Mark. He seemed momentarily stunned. And Mrs. Shaw, the previously protesting, indignant Mrs. Shaw, had somehow been replaced by a warm-eyed, admiring woman. And Papa was still very much who he always was, only more of him. Yes, that was it. He took up more of the room and the air, as if he needed all the oxygen in the room to fuel his enthusiasm.

How charming they were, sitting there in her living room, talking and exchanging glances and touches like they'd been married half their lives. Well, they had been, just not to each other. Still, making it look easy, making it look like they *belonged* there and to each other.

Belonging. Why did Angela crave it and fear it at the same time?

Dorothy spoke again. "We have some other news to share. We're getting married in three weeks."

"So soon?" Mark asked.

"My mother's birthday," Dorothy said, settling the subject.

"We came for another reason. Angela, we know you and Mark are still making plans. Have you decided on a date?" Papa asked.

Mark spoke up. "We'll be talking about that tomorrow."

"We will?" Angela asked. "That's what you wanted to talk about?" She shouldn't have been surprised, yet she was anyway.

"No pressure, dear. We're asking you to consider us."

"What she's trying to say is when you and Mark get married, we'd like to rent your house, if that's something you're agreeable to. Can't say I know what it's like to live in someone else's home, but Dorothy and I have talked about it. We want you and Mark to have the farmhouse to yourself."

Angela didn't know what to say, and by the look on Mark's face, neither did he.

"We'd have a place to live, and you'd have someone taking care of your house. Maybe that would solve both our dilemmas," Dorothy explained in her endearing English accent, which could make news of a root canal sound like an invite to a tea party.

All eyes were on Angela now. This was happening. She and Mark were getting married and, obviously, so were Papa and *Dorothy*. While she could tell Mark was trying to adjust to that new reality, it was her new reality that was taking shape in front of her. What better solution could she ask for?

"Of course you can. What a great idea." She paused, checking Mark's face, then Papa's. "Are you sure this will be okay for you?"

"It'll be a change," Papa said as he stood. "We're going to be getting on our way. I turn in early." He looked at Mark. Angela wasn't sure, but it looked like Papa winked.

"Can't say I know what it'll be like living somewhere else, but it's the right time. The trees are in good hands." He nodded to Mark and smiled at Angela.

After they left, Mark noted the time. "Looks like I better be going too. Are we still on for tomorrow?"

"Sure. Did I hear you earlier? That you want to set a date?"

"I thought we'd talk about it," he said casually.

"Should I be worried?"

"Only if you want to get married in December," he said with a laugh and a good-bye hug.

CHAPTER 18

Mark hadn't been to the chasm in years. As they parked and walked past the covered picnic tables, he reached for Angela's hand. The morning could not have been more crisp and clear. He hoped they could decide on a date today. But that wasn't the real reason he'd brought her here.

He woke at four in the morning with the perfect idea of how to explain the tree-keeper's promise. But now, in the light of day, none of it made sense.

There were two state-parks employees repairing the anchoring chain on one of the trash barrels and a couple with two small children at one of the tables.

He suggested they take Charley's trail around and hike back out through the chasm.

"And your leg will be okay?" Angela asked as she watched Mark walk.

"It's mostly fine," he said. "Not going to slow me down. You know how I've been spending time with Papa this year? Learning all I can about the trees?"

Angela nodded.

"When I became owner of the farm last year, I thought I officially became the keeper of the trees."

"Taking over for Papa," she said.

"Exactly. Or so I thought. Remember for Caroline's birthday she picked out two trees and Papa said they could cause a love match?"

"How could I forget?"

"Right. I couldn't believe there was more to the trees. After all this time, Papa still knew things about the trees he hadn't told me. So I asked him, more like I told him, I wanted to know everything there was to know."

They were a half of a mile down Charley's loop, the rocky path covered in bright orange and red leaves. A thin morning mist hung around the trees. A sparrow chirped and flitted on the ground, then flew to a branch.

"Does this have to do with us setting a date? Are we supposed to get married within a certain amount of time or what—the love expires?" She laughed as she said it, but her words had a nervous edge.

"No. Nothing like that," Mark reassured her. "Well, it does have to do with the trees. But we can get married when we want. When *you* want."

Mark continued. "Angela, the trees have an energy. I've noticed I can feel it. What I mean is, there's only one keeper at a time. And Papa wasn't ready last year."

"Ready for what?" She looked confused and for good reason.

"Let me start over. There's a promise every keeper makes when he becomes *the* keeper. I didn't even know about it. Papa said he wasn't ready last year, but since I asked to know everything there was to know, he said it was time."

"Time for what?"

"Time for me to make the promise."

Their steps were unison, their hands linked by a few fingers. Angela lifted her chin and looked straight ahead on the rocky trail. "What does it mean?"

Mark inhaled, hoping the fresh autumn air would give him the nerve he needed to say it out loud.

"The trees have an energy and feelings. Sometimes I can feel or sense them. It doesn't sound rational, and I'll understand if you don't buy it. I don't know if I would. Maybe that was why it took another year for me to be ready. If I hadn't felt some things, gotten ideas from the trees, I might have thought Papa was making it up."

Angela was quiet.

Mark waited. Was she having second thoughts? "It's not like the trees talk to me or anything. Like Papa says, 'They don't speak English.'" He tried to laugh, but his voice trailed off.

She still didn't say anything.

"Look, do you want some time to think about it? Maybe I should have waited to propose, but I didn't know what I didn't know."

"Have you already made the promise, then?" she asked, but he couldn't tell if there were pain or sadness or confusion in her eyes.

"Yes. It wasn't a big deal, though. I mean it was, but it was just Papa, and I repeated after him, and that was it." Mark listened to his own words, wondering how they sounded to her. His insecurity took over.

"You don't have to marry me. If all this sounds too . . . too far-fetched, I understand. We can call it off."

Angela stopped walking.

"Don't ever say that to me again. Unless *you* don't want to marry *me*. I know I don't *have* to marry you. But I love you. And we are not calling it off." She began walking again.

Mark caught up to her and reached for her hand. He looked into her eyes. "You mean it, don't you?" he asked.

Her eyes were wet. She nodded.

"What do you think about it—about me and the trees?"

"I don't know yet. But when I think of what we've been through together, I can't deny the miracles I've seen. I love you, and I've known from day one that you and the trees were a package deal." She had the faintest of smiles as she said this almost playfully. "Hold on a minute. What exactly did you promise?" she asked.

"To keep the trees from all forms of danger . . . with my body, heart, and mind," he said nonchalantly.

"Just your body, heart, and mind? Is that all?" she asked but even more lighthearted than before. She pointed to his left leg. "So I can expect more of *that*?"

"I don't make a habit of this, no," he said. "But it does mean I'll take care of the trees and land so our family can have a home." He thought of Papa's words to Nana.

They'd come to the end of Charley's loop and could either walk back the way they'd come or hike through the chasm. There was a brook here, usually a small one tucked into the side of a rock wall next to the path. But with the week of heavy rain, it ran fuller and louder and had created a wider path. More like a stream. And by the look of the mud patterns, it had probably been a river last week.

"The sound—I love how loud it is. It has a way of drowning out everything. It clears my head, you know?" Angela said.

"We don't have to hike back through the chasm. We could stay here for a while and go back using the loop trail again." The chasm had some rockier parts—Devil's Coffin and Lover's Leap, not to mention Fat Man's Misery, the tomahawk-sliced rock tunnel. But Angela insisted. Yes, she loved the brook, but she hadn't come all the way to this chasm she'd read about just to turn around and go home without actually seeing it.

On they hiked. Descended, to be more specific. Though only a quarter of a mile in length, some granite walls stretched seventy feet high. They passed by another stream and a good number of felled trees.

They were hiking through the chasm at the perfect time as the granite walls shielded them from full exposure to the sun. It must have been at least ten degrees cooler here.

"The irony isn't lost on me."

"What irony?" Mark asked.

"You bring me to Purgatory Chasm," she said it with a smirk, "to plan our wedding."

"Look, I can't help it if one of the prettiest places in Sutton has the same name as some after-life limbo."

"You mean a state of punishment and suffering."

Mark held up both hands. "You liked the trail and the brook, didn't you? I don't know where they got the name."

"It will be fine. I won't think of it as omen or anything."

"How about you choose the date, then? Fair enough?" Mark asked.

This question came at the same time Angela stepped on some uneven rocks and almost lost her footing. Mark grabbed her arm and held her long enough for her to regain her balance.

"Thanks. What do you mean, me choose? We both need to agree."

Mark waited until Angela had a taken a few more steps and then suggested a double wedding with Papa and Dorothy.

Angela spun around, almost losing her balance again. "Are you out of your mind? That's in two weeks."

"We've known each other four seasons. Wasn't that the requirement?"

"Yes. No. Sort of. I'm not even entertaining this," Angela said with another deliberate step on a rock nearer to the even ground.

"How about November?" he said dryly.

"Mark, be serious. I like your idea of me being able to choose the date. It needs to be sometime next year."

"Next *year*?"

"It's October. That's not as far away as it sounds."

"Fine, if you want a January wedding, it's a little cold, but it could work," Mark said.

Angela stopped and looked at him more closely. "You skipped December? Why not December if you're in such a hurry?"

"Oh, I don't know. It may have something to do with a little tree farm we manage. Even I know better than to try to pull off a wedding in December."

"That's the most sense you've spoken since we started this discussion," Angela said. "Since you proposed to me on the autumnal equinox, what if we get married on the spring equinox? That's in March, isn't it?"

Mark took a drink of water, giving himself time to think. He'd already made up his mind. They would get married on the day *Angela* wanted.

"It's the twentieth. Is that what you want?"

"Most people plan a summer wedding, a June wedding, but June doesn't mean anything to us, does it?"

They stood on a slab of rock on a narrow part of the trail and had to move into the brush to allow a father with several sons to climb past them. The sun was rising higher in the sky.

"That's when we shear the trees."

Angela remembered her shearing accident and shuddered. Mark had only needed three stitches, but still.

"No. Not June. March and the equinox are perfect," she said. "It feels right, doesn't it?"

They took deliberate steps down the side of the trail, being sure to wipe their shoes on the brush and gravel so no wetness accumulated. Flat rocks lived up famously to the cliché "slippery when wet."

The trail opened up to large expanse of a granite slab, half shaded, half warmed by the sun. A retired couple had claimed part of the cooler section, so Mark angled toward the opposite side where there was mostly sun and spotty patches of shade.

"Let's take a rest," Mark said. "I think March will be great. Right before planting season." The month was fine, but something else troubled him.

"Angela, what about your ring? I can buy another one."

"We talked about this. No. You built a music studio *and* dance floor for us."

"For you," he said.

"Exactly."

Mark watched her as she said it. Not a hint of sadness or resentment. "But you need a ring."

"I don't want you to buy a new one. The other ring could still turn up," she said, taking a drink of her water.

Mark wondered if she really believed that. How could she?

"Angela, I had the ring in my pocket during the flood. I waded through sludge. How could it turn up?"

"Let's give it till March. How about that?"

What could Mark say in the face of such optimism? In the face of such beauty?

"I love you," he said.

CHAPTER 19

The farm was only a ten-minute drive on Route 146 from the chasm. Angela watched the trees come into sight through the passenger window. How much her life had changed since she and Caroline had come looking for a Christmas tree last year. She wasn't frantic to pay rent, she had her own home, and she and her mom were on speaking terms. And the most unexpected change of all: Mark in her life, with all his kindness and goodness and love.

She couldn't deny the miracle of their meeting, her heart opening up enough to get to know him better, and the connection of their families. Too many times to count over the last ten months she'd thought of those Shafer miracle trees.

"So was Papa serious about the trees causing love matches?" she asked as they approached the farm.

"I think so. Why do you ask?"

"He said we could have a wedding before Christmas, that's all," Angela said while still staring out the window.

"I'm telling you, November is an option," Mark said playfully.

"Not an option. Two months isn't even enough time to find a dress," Angela said.

"He was putting pressure on me, that's all. Don't let it get to you," Mark insisted. "We decided on March. March twentieth."

"There might still be snow on the ground," she said mostly to herself.

Mark parked his truck, and they were well into the farmhouse when Mark asked why that might be a problem.

"Just thinking about the reception. It would be lovely behind the farmhouse, next to Donna's barn."

"Outside in March it will be too cold," he said. "If we're careful about how many people we invite and empty these two rooms of their furniture, it could work."

Angela turned and looked at him like he had spoken a foreign language. "We'll be getting married at the church downtown. The First Congregational, same one as Papa and Dorothy."

She could tell this surprised Mark. He crossed over to the cash register and seemed interested in some papers on the counter.

"Mark?"

"Okay. Sure," he said.

His sudden disinterest in the topic raised her suspicions.

"Are you sure it's okay?"

"I thought you'd said your mother had insisted on a big church wedding before with—and that you didn't want that again."

With Todd. It's what he was about to say. But he hadn't.

"You're right. I did say that. But the important word there is *big*. Our church wedding will be small, with the people who know and love us. Much more intimate."

He didn't respond right away. Papa and Dorothy came through the side door, speaking to each other and laughing. They looked up, and Dorothy's eyes met Angela's. She looked back and forth between her and Mark.

"Alberto, come with me to the barn."

"But you said you wanted to start fixin' dinner."

"And I will—after we visit the barn. We should check on Caroline and see how her painting is coming along," she said, giving Papa a stern look.

They walked out the front door.

Mark shuffled the mail and some papers and finally said, "Maybe it's for the best. With all the time we spend here, why not have the ceremony somewhere else?"

The tone in Mark's voice bothered Angela all the way home. His concession seemed forced and insincere—something Mark usually never was. And why had he assumed the wedding would take place at the farm? Couldn't he have asked her what she thought?

But then again, she hadn't asked him what he thought.

Caroline broke her out of her self-absorbed ruminations.

"Mom, look at what I made today with Mrs. Shaw." Caroline held up a miniature ceramic house. The hand-painted sign above the door read "Ice Cream Shoppe."

"It has this space in the back. We can put a light in there so light will shine in the windows. Can it go on the table by the sofa?"

"Sure, but we'll have to put it near an outlet," Angela said.

"Or maybe on the kitchen counter by the phone. We can have a little bit of Christmas in every room!"

Angela smiled to herself. Knowing Caroline, she'd change her mind three times before Christmas anyway.

"Remember you wanted them to go under the tree?" Angela asked.

"Yes, but since we only have these two, it won't be much of a village," Caroline said.

"Funny you should say that."

"What does that mean?" her daughter asked with growing excitement.

"What would you say if Mrs. Shaw gave us a few more pieces?"

"I'd say I love Mrs. Shaw! That's awesome. Wait, I have something," she said as she ran to her room and back, yelling to no one in particular that Christmas was going to rock!

When she returned, she showed her mother a small hand mirror. "We can use this for a lake. And Mrs. Shaw said she had some batting stuff that could look like snow. Also, maybe a place in the center for the nativity!"

"Like Bethlehem?" Angela asked, trying to keep up with her daughter's excitement.

Caroline gasped. "Bethlehem! Mom, you're so right. This can be the little town of Bethlehem."

"You know that Bethlehem didn't have snow, right?" Angela cautioned.

"Who cares," she said.

Angela should have seen that one coming. Even if Caroline was missing the point, she wasn't going to be deterred if the village houses resembled something from a Norman Rockwell painting circa 1920, rather than an ancient Middle-Eastern town like Bethlehem. Obviously they weren't striving for historical accuracy.

"Also, there are a few more pieces left to paint."

"I'll take care of that!"

Angela picked up the mail and sat in her wicker chair on the screened porch. A few bills, a neighborhood coupon book, and a picture of a fountain and flowers. She turned the postcard over—the Botanical Garden in Cologne, Germany.

Hi, Angela,

I have a few minutes before I go down for breakfast. I could eat in my room, but there is something to getting up and dressed every day that is supposed to help with the jet lag. I had hoped the six-hour time difference wouldn't be this disorienting.

We visited the Botanical Garden yesterday. We tour the Picasso collection tomorrow—not my favorite, but I will not leave Cologne without seeing it. And today we'll visit the chocolate museum.

I want my money back for those French lessons—no one could understand a word I said when we visited Marseille. Whenever I spoke, people looked at me either very confused or with great alarm. Nancy says my German is much better than my French, but so far everyone here speaks English with me. Which is a great relief. I didn't account for conjugating verbs while jet-lagged.

Hope you and Caroline are well. Are you still engaged? Do you have a date? A ring?

Yours truly,
Mother

Angela turned the card over and stared at the gardens, so lush and manicured. She turned it back over and reread her mother's words.

A date? A ring? Half a world away with everything she's ever wanted to see and she is still trying to plan my wedding.

But then again, maybe these weren't controlling, pressure-filled questions. Maybe she truly cared.

There wasn't time to figure it out. She had to help Caroline get ready for Papa and Dorothy's wedding.

As she stashed the mail by her purse on the counter, she saw the small slip of paper from her trip to the beach. She pulled it out—the phone number for Florinda's cousin. She'd already had it for a month and hadn't called. It *had* been a busy month, with "little" things like a flood, getting engaged, and sending her mother off to Europe.

But what she wouldn't give to hear Florinda's voice. To talk to her. Why? She didn't know all the reasons she meant so much to her. As her piano teacher for five years, they certainly spent many hours together during her lessons, but it was more than that. Florinda had sincerely cared about her. She had taken the time to get to know what Angela did and didn't like. She not only knew what her talents were, she believed in her. And the more she thought about it, Angela could remember the feeling of having someone care about her dreams, the feeling of having someone want her happiness, *her* dreams to come true.

Maybe they could talk and she could tell her about Mark and the farm and the trees. She knew how Florinda would smile if she told her she was happy for the first time in a long time. Or maybe for the first time ever.

She looked at the number again. *Would Florinda be as happy to talk to me as I would be to talk to her? After all, she hasn't reached out to me in all these years.*

They were ugly, unbidden thoughts, but they did the trick. She folded the paper and put it back in her purse. Maybe another time.

Angela and Mark entered the church with slowing steps. Their conversation on the drive had hovered between strained and nonexistent. Mark hadn't reached for her hand. She hadn't reached for his. But here they were, entering the church for Papa's wedding to Dorothy.

Or as she'd soon be called, Mrs. Shafer.

Mrs. Shafer.

The name struck Angela with a bit of force, followed by an unexpected longing.

Angela pushed it aside. She was here to think about Papa and

Dorothy, not herself, even if Dorothy were officially joining the Shafer family before she was. She would be happy for her *and* Papa.

They sat on the front pew next to Caroline, who was smoothing her dress over her knees. She'd come with Dorothy at her insistence: "For company, so I don't lose my wits altogether today."

Angela settled into the bench, noticing the carved wood of the pulpit and the height of the organ pipes. There was a smell of new carpet and old wood. The autumn morning sun sent a yellow hue streaming through the stained-glass windows.

The center window depicted Jesus with Martha and Mary. Angela knew that much. And maybe if she thought about it long enough, that Jesus had said, "Mary had chosen that good part," but the wedding was about to begin.

Mark leaned forward and winked at Caroline, then sat up straight against the bench.

Angela's heart softened at the sight of him, always so thoughtful of Caroline.

They watched and listened and cried. Well, Angela cried. She wasn't sure about anyone else. She waited until Papa and the new Mrs. Shafer were out of the chapel before she turned to Mark. "I'm sorry for ever suggesting we wait four seasons." She said it as directly to Mark as she could so that Caroline would not overhear.

A slow and mischievous smile spread across Mark's face. "So what you're saying is before we leave here today, we should talk to the pastor and reserve the church?"

"No, there's no need to do that." Angela held eye contact. "There is only one place we should say our vows, you and I." She paused. "Do you think that little tree farm, the one with the miracle trees, do you think it's booked next March?"

Mark's eyes widened. He stopped in the aisle and hugged her. Then he lifted her up and spun her around before returning her to her feet.

CHAPTER 20

From the moment they left the church after Papa's wedding, Mark had been hard at work getting the farm and the trees ready for opening weekend. The day after Thanksgiving always came quick, but with the flood cleanup this year, it felt like it had come that much earlier. Four weeks had hardly been enough. He and Brett and their seasonal employees spent hours on grading the land, leveling the places that had been altered by the flood. The sales lot was finally walkable, but the inventory of saleable trees was low. Yet Mark felt at peace. On his morning walks among the trees, peace had filled his heart more than once. These were walks he'd taken alone, without Papa.

It shouldn't have surprised Mark, but Papa had told him not to expect to see him in the mornings. He'd even quoted Deuteronomy. Something about a man with a new wife not going out to war or being charged with any business, but instead being free to be at home one year.

"One year?" Mark had challenged, though the idea did sound tempting.

Papa had laughed. "We'll settle for two weeks."

The last customers left the tree lot. Brett closed out the register. Mrs. Shaw, Dorothy, was still in the craft barn with Angela and Caroline. Mark hadn't seen Papa for a while. Usually he stayed on the lot till closing, but not tonight. Mark searched for him inside. He approached the back office and found Papa sitting at the desk, writing.

"There you are. I didn't see you come in. Can I help you?"

"No," Papa said and continued writing.

Mark crossed the room, pretending to search for something in the filing cabinet. He could come right out and ask Papa what he was doing, but he waited. It might be better if Papa volunteered the information.

"How'd we do tonight?" Papa asked without looking up.

"We moved about half of the front lot of trees. That's about what we do every year this time, maybe a little better," Mark said. "Everything okay?"

"Yep," Papa said.

Mark exhaled.

"But what you're trying to ask is 'What the dickens am I doing at your desk,' right?"

"Right." Mark laughed.

"Leaving you my address."

"Address?"

"Dorothy's daughter's address. She and I leave for Oregon tomorrow."

"A trip now? Before Christmas?"

"We are still newlyweds. Better now than during Christmas, don't you think?" Papa said with a wink. He pushed back from the desk and stood. "You've got things well under control around here. Besides, it's better for you and the trees if I'm gone for a while."

"But this is the busiest time of year." Mark sat down in the chair opposite. It wasn't just the customers and the holiday. It was Papa. For all the training and the keeper's promise, he'd never looked forward to the day when he would work the farm without him. Especially not for a strangely-timed honeymoon.

"Dorothy's daughter is having her baby any day now. Can't argue with the grandchild's arrival plans."

Ah. Mark had heard Mrs.—Dorothy talk about the baby. She'd even mentioned visiting after she was born. That was before she and Papa married, and Mark hadn't paid very good attention to when that was happening. Apparently it was happening now.

Papa walked out of the office and Mark followed.

Brett waved good night and left as Angela, Caroline, and Dorothy were coming through the side door. A flurry of snow came in with them.

"I'll be much warmer than this soon," Dorothy said, fussing with the scarf around her neck.

"Do you know when you'll be coming back? Will you be here for Christmas?" Mark asked. Why did he feel anxious about this?

Papa stopped midstride and turned to look at Mark. Dorothy had heard the question.

A moment of unusual tension filled the room.

Mark looked to Papa and then to Dorothy. And then to Angela, who was already shaking her head in a subtle but furious way.

"This is my Mandy's fourth baby, Mark. She's going to need all the help I can give her."

Mark didn't say anything else. Papa and Dorothy retreated to the master bedroom. Something Mark was not at all used to. He went and sat in the chair near the fireplace and could hear Caroline asking Angela about what just happened.

He sat thinking of Christmas at the farm without Papa and how it didn't feel right. Or maybe he didn't want it to feel right.

Caroline interrupted his deliberations.

"Mark, my mom says a sleepover on Christmas Eve is out of the question." She came and sat cross-legged in front of the fireplace. "But we can come on Christmas Day, right?"

"Caroline, we'll come for dinner, like we did last year," Angela said.

Mark had an idea. "Caroline, maybe if Papa and Dorothy don't come back for the holiday, you and your mom can stay here and I'll stay in the cabin. How about that?" He looked to Angela expecting approval, feeling like he'd found a way for Caroline to have her Christmas wish.

Only, Angela's eyes were stern, and she folded her arms across her chest.

"That's a great idea. Can we, Mom? Can we?" Caroline hopped up from the floor and ran and pulled her mom closer into the sitting area by the fireplace.

Mark smiled, recognizing that reluctant attitude, knowing she wouldn't be able to resist the offer for long.

Angela looked at Caroline. "Looks like you might get your

THE TREE KEEPER'S PROMISE

Christmas wish after all, young lady." She hugged her, and as they separated, Angela asked, "What is it about being here on Christmas Day?"

"There won't be anyone here but us, right, Mark?" Caroline asked.

"Right," Mark answered.

"I thought if no one were around, you wouldn't mind if I pretended to be keeper for the day. You know, keeper of the trees."

Keeper for the day. Why hadn't he thought of it before? A day for kids to act as keeper and learn about the trees. Mark decided to offer it on Saturdays with the hot dog and hayride event. With Papa out of town, Brett agreed to give the hayrides so Mark could run the first group of "keepers-in-training." If there was a good response, they could develop this program throughout the year. A way to reach out to the community.

One step at a time.

Brett brought the mail to Mark, who was in the back office taking care of a few business items before the day's activities began.

"You may want to take a look at this." He handed him a letter. Mark could see it was from the Department of Transportation.

"Speeding tickets?" Brett asked.

"I wish that's all it was," Mark answered. He held the envelope, thinking of the children who would be coming to the farm today, not wanting to have this weighing on his mind.

"What are you waiting for?"

Mark tore into it, then scanned the first few lines. His heart sank.

"After extensive research and planning . . . property has been identified . . . facilitate the expansion of Route 146."

There was more information about a community information meeting, but he folded the paper and put it in the desk drawer.

"Was it something I said?" Brett asked.

No sense in keeping it a secret. "MassDOT did a futures study. When they expand 146, they want to build a new ramp and a frontage road."

"And why the letter to you?"

"They want to put the frontage road through the south lot of trees."

"Can they do that?" Brett asked.

Mark stood up from the desk, thinking of the families arriving at the farm as they spoke. "Usually property owners don't have a choice in the matter." He handed the letter back to Brett. "But I intend to change that."

CHAPTER 21

Helping Dorothy with the crafts and the barn was how Angela imagined spending December, not running the entire place by herself. But with Dorothy across the country in Oregon, that was exactly what she was in for.

"Would you do that for me? Keep the shelves stocked, and straight too, after the little ones come through? It would mean so much to me," Dorothy had asked.

It seemed like the least she could do.

"There's not much to it," she'd said.

Not much to it. Until the Putnam Bed-and-Breakfast ordered ten handmade pine wreaths—nine small ones for each of their windows and one large one for their door. And seventy-five custom-cut wood ornaments.

In between cutting wire for the wreaths and tying red ribbons onto each wood snowflake, Angela helped customers. It only took a few minutes to ring up their orders, but she soon learned that the customers liked to visit. Some were new to the area, some were getting a real tree for the first time, and some had been coming to the farm for over thirty years.

One such customer, Ilene, set down her items, reached over the counter, and greeted Angela with a two-armed hug. "I heard about you and Mark. We couldn't be more thrilled. Welcome to the neighborhood." The woman turned before she left, and added, "His mom and dad would be so happy. We're all happy for you both."

After Ilene left the barn, Angela picked up a wooden snowflake, tied another ribbon to it, and thought about the extended farm family Mark often talked about. She remembered her parent's friends, mostly political friends, and how they would try to get close to her and their family.

But this felt different. In fact, it might take some getting used to—people treating her like they'd known her as long as they'd known Mark. Treating her with a two-armed-hug kind of love.

Caroline burst through the doors and ran to where Angela was working on a wreath.

"Mom. Do you get to take a break? You have to come see what we've been doing," she said, a bit breathless.

"There's someone coming in an hour. Can you give me a hint?"

"Mice. Did you know mice can be a problem for the trees, even in the winter?" She picked up a pine branch and waved it emphatically as she talked. "We—the kids who came today to be "keepers"—we helped Mark put this mesh stuff around some of the trees."

Angela nodded, noticing Caroline's rosy cheeks and happy eyes.

"That was more than a hint. But you still need to come see. And you know what else he's been teaching us? Did you know if you take the bark off a tree it could die? I remember reading about it in science last year, but I get it now. Mark explained how the trees need nutrients and grow from the roots to the leaves. The leaves turn the nutrients into sugar, or something like it, and send it back to the roots. If you take off the bark—see, it protects the living part of the tree—it will stop the system."

"So you like being a keeper for the day?"

"Yes." She gave Angela a hug and said, "I could be the keeper every day!" She ran between the craft shelves, yelling, "And Mark says we can get our trees in a few days. Maybe sooner if it means that much to me. Those were his words, not mine."

With that, she was out the door.

When Angela and Caroline arrived at the farm, the cloudless sky showed off the white-blue winter sunrise. Temperatures had dropped ten degrees below the average, but they held out hope that it would get above freezing. Caroline wore an extra layer of clothes and her favorite scarf. Angela wore her wool socks and warmest boots. She could handle most anything about the cold, unless it got to her feet. As long as her toes stayed warm, she was fine.

Mark was sitting on the porch waiting for them as they pulled in. She could see him slightly reclined, his arm draped around the empty chair beside him. He wore a hat she was sure Dorothy had knitted.

She felt that swirl in her stomach, and the corners of her mouth turned up. She wasn't sure what warmed her heart more—seeing him there or picturing herself sitting next to him. In the summer they could enjoy the late evening breeze after a humid day. In the fall they could watch Caroline jump in a pile of leaves. In the winter they could come to the porch for some star-gazing on a clear night. In the spring they could rest after a long day of planting. Every season, Angela realized. She could picture herself with Mark in every season.

How did that happen?

They hiked to the lots of six- and seven-year old trees—the Scotch pines Mark had showed them in September. Caroline was even more bouncy than she had been on that day, if it were possible. Angela would have thought the cold might have subdued her energy, but, no, she ran ahead of them, stopping at every third or fourth tree before moving on.

"I think she's waited for this day all year," Angela said to Mark.

"Maybe I have too," he said as he took her hand.

"Cutting down another tree? That's not anything new, is it?"

They walked another step or two before Mark responded.

"Maybe putting one up."

"That hasn't lost its excitement?"

"Just the opposite. I'm more excited this year about the tree than I've ever been," Mark said, then he called to Caroline. "This way. Over here." They turned to the right, down another row of trees.

"Why is that?" Angela asked.

"I have an idea. How about you and Caroline move over to the farmhouse now? No reason to wait until the holiday."

"Where will you be?" she asked hesitantly.

"I'll stay in the cabin. I feel the same way you do about Caroline, about us. Cold as the cabin is, I'll stay there and keep my distance." He exuded self-control as he said it. A frustratingly attractive kind of self-control.

"When will Papa and Dorothy come back?"

"Not for several more weeks."

Angela knew from what Dorothy had told her that they might not even be back for Christmas.

"I'll think about it," Angela said, knowing Caroline would love it. But that was also the reason for her reservations. Whenever Papa and Dorothy returned, they'd need to move back out, and March was still three months away.

The path underfoot became harder, rockier. The ground had frozen rivulets in it. The trees—she looked at the lower branches and caught her breath. So many of them were damaged or gone.

"Mark, I hadn't realized."

"These two rows had it the worst," he said.

They approached Caroline standing by the next row of trees. It appeared her extra energy had subsided. This section of trees fared somewhat better than the other rows they passed, but the trees still showed scars where the water had ripped through them.

"This is our tree. See the polka-dot ribbon?" She said it calmly, seeming a bit sad.

"Caroline, I'm so sorry," Angela said. So many of the branches were mangled and broken.

"It's all right. Lights and ornaments will help."

"Where is the other tree you chose?"

They looked for the sunflower. Caroline walked right to it. "This is the one for your house, Mark."

Angela could see right away this one had the most damage of the two. Its top branches looked wind-whipped. "Why don't we pick out another tree for the farmhouse? This one looks so battered. And we need one to look good for the customers." Angela looked to Mark for confirmation, only he was looking at Caroline, not at any of the trees.

"But this is the tree. This is the one. You still like it, right,

Mark?" Caroline wiped her eyes with the back of her mittened hand.

Mark motioned to Angela with his eyebrows before he spoke again. "If this tree is good enough for you, Caroline, it's good enough for the farm. And just fine with me."

"Can we put it up tonight?" she asked.

Though they hadn't planned to, Angela looked at Mark, who nodded. Neither of them was a match for Caroline's sadness.

"That's fine with me," Mark said to Caroline, then, more to Angela, he said, "I know we were going to cut your tree and get it over to your house today. I was going to come back for the farmhouse tree. But if you're okay with putting this one up tonight, I can bring your tree over in a day or two."

She knew he was asking about logistics and being considerate of what they had planned. And she knew that Caroline was only thinking of being able to make that poor little tree look beautiful, but she thought about Mark's earlier invitation of moving in and Caroline's love of the farm and the trees. What was she worried about?

"We may only need one tree after all this year." She said it to Mark, but Caroline quickly caught on to her meaning.

"Do you mean it? One tree for the farmhouse?" she asked.

"We'll stay there until Papa and Dorothy get back. Mark will be in the cabin. How does that sound?"

"Sounds awesome!" Caroline said.

"It's not too late if you want to pick out a better tree, one that wasn't hit as hard."

"Mom, it's like what you tell me to do at school. Choose my friends and then be a friend." She walked up closer to the tree and touched a bare spot on the trunk, then ran her hand along one of the branches. "I chose this tree, and now I want to be its friend."

For as cold as it had been as they'd trekked through the trees, the farmhouse was every bit as warm. Mark had started a fire, and they'd made hot chocolate, and when Angela told Mark they liked to listen to Christmas music as they decorated, he queued up a playlist in the studio. Though the dining room was between them and the dance floor, the sound carried and filled the house with a festive air. Just what they needed.

Angela and Caroline had gone home to pack and bring over enough clothes for a few weeks. Angela also grabbed her one box of tree decorations, thinking it was slightly ironic that she was bringing even that much to help decorate their tree. Surely between the inventory at the barn and what Dorothy had already set aside for the farm tree, there was more than could fit on what branches were left on this tree.

This felt like more than a decorating project. Mark and Angela were sharing this tree, creating a new family, creating a new tradition. So, yes, they needed her musical ornaments and Caroline's baby-picture ones.

Caroline had asked—no, begged—to bring the village houses. Though Angela wasn't sure how Mark would feel about their growing makeshift town of Bethlehem taking over a good portion of the living room, her daughter's pleading convinced her.

Angela settled into the sofa while Mark and Caroline worked around the tree. She handed out the ornaments and beads and the popcorn strings Dorothy had made. Mark kept up with Caroline's excitement over every piece and finding "just the right spot" on the tree.

As they finished, Mark centered the angel on top and then went and turned down the room lights. He disappeared into the studio, and soon a new track of "O Tannenbaum" began to play.

"If Papa were here, he'd sing this for us," Mark said when he returned.

"Mom, now that the tree is up, do you think we'll have a wedding before Christmas?" Caroline asked with wide eyes.

"Hold on a second. Papa and Dorothy are married, and Mark and I are engaged. I think that settles it."

"But Papa was talking about your wedding."

Angela asked Mark for a little help.

"Papa likes to have fun," Mark said. "This is the busiest month of the year here. How about we set up your village now?"

She agreed, and they each took pieces and began arranging them under the tree.

"Papa will be glad to see this," Mark said. "When he was boy, he was in charge of setting up the village every year. Donna would decorate our tree, but we haven't had anyone to do the village."

After the toy shop and church were positioned, as well as the ice cream parlor and blacksmith shop, Caroline put some of the white batting in place around her mirror. She had collected small pebbles—from where, Angela didn't know—and made a cobblestone road to the church.

"We're calling this Bethlehem, Mark," Caroline said. "Our very own."

"I've told her it didn't snow there," Angela said lightly.

Mark nodded. "I like it."

"What about our nativity?" Caroline asked. "Have you showed it to Mark? How about we put it in the village? That would help it."

Angela loved the idea. So what if the scale were off and if the houses were ceramic and the nativity was made of carved wood? All the better. But they were quickly running out of space if they were going to keep it out of the way of customer foot traffic.

"What about the fireplace mantel? That might be safer."

"Not up there. Can I move the bakery and schoolhouse? Please, Mom?"

As Caroline asked, Mark lifted pieces out of the velvet lined box and handed them to her. She eagerly began telling Mark what Angela had told her about each piece. The very things that she learned last year—what Florinda had taught Angela.

"Have a pure heart like Mary," Caroline repeated. "And this lamb—Jesus knows all the names of his lambs and He finds the lost ones."

Okay, they weren't Florinda's exact words, but close.

"Do we have room for all of them?" Caroline asked.

"Of course. We'll *make* the room," Mark said. He handed her the Wise Men and the animals.

Mark's words triggered another memory of Florinda.

They were in Angela's childhood home, standing by the door as Florinda was leaving. Florinda scanned the house and asked Angela where she would put up the new nativity set she'd given her. Angela remembered looking around. Her mother's things filled the space. Vases and statues and pictures. Crystal clocks and fancy dishes. Elegant pieces of art. "I don't know. I'll ask my mom," Angela had told her.

Florinda became quite serious. "You must make room, my Angela. Not only here"—she made a sweeping motion with her hand—"but here," then placed her hand over her heart. "This is how we show love, my little lamb, we make room here."

Angela focused on Caroline. She was setting up the last piece of their nativity under the freshly cut and decorated tree she'd chosen, the one she insisted they keep. Mark was sitting on the floor next to her, fine-tuning the arrangement.

We'll make room.

"Here, Mark." Caroline had taken a piece from the nativity. "You need something for the cabin. Take this lamb." With that, she gave him a quick hug and ran down the hall to bed. She and Angela would share the master bedroom until they could fix up the smaller room with a twin bed.

Mark and Angela lingered by the side door. He gently moved her dark curls over her shoulder and pulled her close for a hug. He kissed her cheek and said good night.

"That's it?" she asked before she could stop herself.

"I'm pretty sure she's still awake," Mark said. "She's probably peeking at us right now."

"No, I'm not," Caroline called from the room.

They both laughed. "How she can hear us, I'll never know," Angela said.

After Mark left, Angela cleaned up some of the packaging and boxes. It was just her and the tree and some music.

Sweet tones of "O Little Town of Bethlehem" drifted to where Angela sat by the fire, a clear view of the angel-topped tree and the very first "Shafer-Bethlehem" town below.

"How still we see thee lie."

The memorable words cheered her. As the third verse played, she listened more closely to words that were not as familiar to her.

How silently, how silently,
The wondrous Gift is giv'n!
So God imparts to human hearts
The blessings of His heaven.
No ear may hear His coming,
But in this world of sin,
Where meek souls will receive Him still,
The dear Christ enters in.

Angela's heart swelled. Florinda's words "We make room here" returned, and then Mark's: "We'll make the room."

She had simply wanted to surprise her daughter with a new

tradition for their family. Maybe she should have known Caroline would want an entire village. But she couldn't have known that assembling a hodgepodge of ceramic houses to recreate their own little Bethlehem would make room in her heart for belonging, room for love. And room for Mark.

CHAPTER 22

Mark strolled to the cabin in the still night air, crunching pine needles underfoot and thinking of the cute look on Angela's face after he kissed her cheek.

"*That's it?*" she'd asked. What he wouldn't give to hold her a little tighter, kiss her a little longer.

March could not come soon enough.

He turned on the light in his bedroom and set the lamb Caroline had given him on the dresser. She had been so excited to give it to him. Excited to decorate and set up a village. It was a year ago that he'd met Angela and Caroline for the first time, and yet it felt like he'd known them much longer. It felt like they had been part of the farm forever and that they belonged together.

He picked up his guitar and sang as he played. Angela's song. *Maybe this can be her Christmas gift.*

With customers at the farm and Papa in Oregon, Mark hadn't had much time to follow up with the Historical Society. When Mrs. Simmons called to tell him she had something for the farm, he didn't hesitate to go see her.

It was late afternoon when he returned to the farmhouse. Brett was helping customers, Angela was with Caroline in the farmhouse, and one of their seasonal employees was helping in Donna's barn. Mark immediately began moving things behind the cash register—a printer, a letter tray, a decorative basket with gold pinecones. Then he pounded a nail into the wall and called for Angela and Caroline to come see what he was doing.

"What's all this?" Angela asked.

"A little something for the farm."

He held up an oval, bronze plaque with the inscription "The Shafer Farm, 1881. This property has been placed on the National Register of Historic Places by the United States Department of the Interior."

"Congratulations! That's great news!" Angela said and gave him a hug.

Before Caroline could say anything, some customers came through the front door of the farmhouse.

They turned to greet them. Mark's jaw dropped. John Jackson stood there with his arm around . . .

"Ashley?" Angela exclaimed. "How—why . . . I mean, what are you doing here?"

"John and I had a late lunch." She glanced at him with a smirk. "We thought we'd come say hi. John says he's been trying to reach Mark."

"That's right. Wanted to check on the tree for the Auburn mall. Did that work out?"

Mark nodded and chose his words carefully. "We delivered a thirty-foot noble fir to them last week. They were very happy."

"Great. Glad to hear it."

Mark was actually about to thank John for the business, but John continued.

"I'm telling you, Mark, I'm on your side. I hate to see someone as hardworking as you lose this place to the Department of Transportation. What do you say we sit down this week and work out the details? I have a respectable deal to offer you."

He and Ashley moved closer to the cash register.

Respectable? Did he just say that?

Mark uncrossed his arms and pointed nonchalantly to the plaque. "Take a look, John. Actually, take one long, last look. We're on the list. *The* list. This plaque means that MassDOT will revise their plans. And so long as I'm alive, it means no one else will own this farm. It will be here for a very, very long time." He remained leaning with his side against the wall and crossed his arms back over his chest.

"How did you pull it off? That's amazing. I know people who've waited years and were denied." John turned on his heel and surveyed the room. He looked at Mark one last time. "This one got away from me, but I gotta say I'm glad to see it in your hands. I have a lot of respect for you, Mark. You're a rare breed. I don't know—it's like you have some kind of connection to these trees," he said. He turned to Ashley. "I've got a client at four thirty. We better go," he said and they prepared to leave.

Mark watched him, allowing a sense of satisfaction to settle over him. He could be rid of John Jackson. But before he reached the door, Mark had a thought. He could let him leave and be done with him for good. Or . . .

"Hey, John," he said casually. John turned around. "If you're ever in town and need a tree, you know where to come."

CHAPTER 23

Angela set the phone down and scanned the living room, not looking at anything directly. Caroline was in Donna's barn, and she was planning to go over and help there soon. But this call from her mother was unexpected.

Though Angela knew the flight had arrived earlier that morning, she also knew her mother would be spending the next several days recuperating from jet lag.

To hear that she was on her way to the farm and that she had something very important that couldn't wait left Angela with a fair amount of dread.

"How important?" Angela had asked.

"What kind of a question is that? I'm so tired. I can't explain it all to you, but it's very, very important."

"Can it wait until you've slept for a day or two? I don't mind. It's been a long day, and I know how you feel about driving all the way to Sutton on a regular day, never mind the same day you've crossed the Atlantic," Angela said with growing concern over what kind of gift she could have possibly brought home.

"It cannot wait," Cathy said with that characteristic tone that left no room for argument.

Angela waited for an explanation. A hint. What could it be?

"So it's perishable?" Angela asked.

"You could say that," Cathy said.

"Like the cereus of gifts? Blooms one night a year and if I miss it it's over?"

"Close, but not quite," Cathy said. "I'm not giving you any more information. Only that I'll be at the farm by three and trust that you'll be there, and Caroline."

"And Mark. I'm guessing you don't want him to miss this?"

"Most definitely Mark."

Right.

As Angela replayed the conversation, she scrutinized her mother's voice, intonation—anything that would give it away. And she still had no clue.

She found Mark on the sales lot and repeated it all to him, exasperated.

"I know it's one of the busiest days of the year for you. If there were anything I could do to put her off, I would. I think she might be bringing me a new truck, but I'm sure she didn't buy that in Europe. And it's not exactly perishable."

"You don't need to put her off," Mark said. "I have an idea of what she's bringing you."

"You do? What?"

"Think about it. She's bringing it to the farm," Mark said.

"So."

"It has to be a tree, probably one from France or Germany. Where else did she go?"

"A tree? We have enough of those. And it's December. How would we plant it?"

"We can keep it in the greenhouse until spring. Remember, she's doing this for you, maybe for us. No matter what it is, let's just go with it."

He's right, she thought. *He's always right about her.*

"Go with it, huh?" she muttered.

"Okay?" Mark pressed.

"Fine," Angela answered.

Angela and Caroline walked from the barn to the farmhouse, bracing themselves against the blustery weather. While the latest storm had not lived up to snowfall predictions, it made up for it with wind and cold temperatures. This did not keep Caroline from bubbling over with excitement to see her grandmother. Angela wasn't sure she wanted to tell her that Grandma Cathy was coming with a gift. Especially without knowing it's nature.

Unless Mark was right, as he usually was.

"Grandma may have a surprise for us."

"Of course she will," Caroline stated.

"How do you know that?"

"It's her way," Caroline said. "Most of the time you don't know what she thinks of you, but then bam!—she gives you something you love and you wonder how she even does it."

Out of the mouths of babes.

"Maybe she went and got you a ring," Caroline said.

"She better not have." Angela's stomach churned at the thought. That would not go over well with Mark, or her, for that matter. "Mark thinks it's a tree, probably a very special one. So let's be excited about it, whatever it is."

The door opened and in walked a tired-looking Cathy. Beside her walked a woman, short in stature, her dark hair pulled to a bun at the back of her neck with gray strands at the edges of her temples. She wore a long winter coat and red leather boots. When she saw Angela—the woman's eyes widened, a smile broke out, and her little legs flew toward her.

"My Angela! Meu cordeirinho," she said in the same accented voice Angela remembered.

"Florinda?" Angela's voice cracked.

As they embraced, Angela looked for her mother. Cathy was watching this unfold with glossy eyes. Angela shook her head in utter disbelief.

"You're not a tree," Caroline said. Only Mark and Angela laughed. Everyone else looked on.

"This must be your daughter?" Florinda said. "She has your likeness when you were a girl."

"And this is Mark, my mom's fiancé," Caroline said.

"How very nice to meet you, Mark. May I?" Florinda gestured toward a chair by the fireplace before sitting. "It is this reason I come now." Her face shone with a bright smile, though it did show some travel weariness.

"For the holiday?" Angela asked.

"No, I must return to Portugal before Christmas."

"I don't understand."

"I come for you and for your Mark." She reached for Angela's hands. "Your mother say you are getting married. Yes, yes? I come for your wedding. Then I can go back."

Mark heard the words. He was sure he had heard them. "*I come for your wedding.*" It may have been broken English, but the woman had clearly said, "*Your mother say you are getting married.*"

This should be interesting.

He hadn't taken his eyes off Angela. He'd watched her surprised expression change to pure joy and then to shock, and possibly fright. Now she was glaring at Cathy, who was almost sobbing. Almost, because that woman had as much composure as the Queen's guard. The thing was, Mark couldn't tell if she was happy to see Angela and Florinda reunited—or if she knew those were flames coming out of Angela's ears.

No one had spoken yet. Just three teary-eyed women all looking at each other—and probably for different reasons.

Just when Mark decided he should take Caroline to find a snack in the kitchen, Angela stepped back and looked straight at him.

Bewildered. Completely bewildered, if Mark had to guess.

"Next Friday morning," Cathy said. "Florinda returns."

"Could you excuse us for a moment?" Angela asked calmly.

They found refuge in the kitchen. Angela took to pacing from one end to the other, stopping at the refrigerator, spinning around, and marching to the cabinets.

"She did it. She really did it," Angela huffed.

"She found Florinda. It's amazing!" Mark said, pretty sure that wasn't what she was referring to but hoping the mention could ease her nerves.

"I know! Do you know how much I've wanted you to meet Florinda and for her to meet you?"

"Seems like your mother did." Mark smiled. Maybe this wouldn't be so bad.

"Oh, my mother. She's going to get her way. I can't believe it. How does she do it?"

"What *way*? What do you mean?"

"What do I mean? Don't play dumb here. That mother of

mine has been trying to set the date for our wedding before we were even engaged. And here we are. Getting married next Thursday."

"Whoa, wait. Next Thursday? Says who? That's two days before Christmas." Mark hadn't moved from the spot where he'd been leaning against the sink, about the midpoint of Angela's pacing track. But now he stood straight, his weight no longer on the counter.

"Good thing you're catching on, since you're the groom here," Angela said dryly, still pacing, still steaming.

"You're not serious? Cathy's not serious? It's December, remember?"

"Mark, that sweet woman flew all the way from Portugal to attend my wedding. You think I'm going to let her go back without seeing it?" Angela didn't stop pacing. This wasn't up for discussion.

"You *are* serious. But—"

"But what? 'Let's just go with it.' Remember saying that?"

"Yes, but—"

"No matter what she brings, right?" Angela asked.

"Right, but this isn't a tree. This isn't a knickknack from Germany or a purse from Italy."

"Exactly, Mark. Welcome to my life. No, wait—our life."

"Angela, I don't see how we can pull off a wedding by next week! You said yourself it takes months."

"We don't have months, Mark. We have days. About four of them."

Mark stretched his arms out, palms up, as if to plead with some mysterious kitchen appliance deity.

Angela stopped directly in front of Mark, tears welling up in her eyes.

Mark stopped thinking of the farm and customers and the holiday and wrapped his arms around Angela instead. He pulled her close and let her sob.

He smoothed back her hair and whispered in her ear.

"How about we get married next week. Right here, with our friends and family. A small, sweet ceremony. Anything you want. It may even be the winter solstice. What do you say to that?"

Angela pulled away enough to search Mark's face. She did that when she was trying to figure him out, it seemed. More tears tumbled from her eyes as she nodded.

"I'll go ahead and call Papa, give him the good news," Mark said when it had been quiet for a moment.

Angela lifted her head. "Oh no. When are they coming back? They were going to spend the holiday with Dorothy's daughter," she said.

Mark could see another storm of tears threatening. "Let's call them right now. Maybe they can find a flight."

Papa answered, and Mark related the events of the day and how, as of that moment, they were planning a wedding for next Thursday. "Could they make it?" he asked, understanding it would be costly to change their flights. When he hung up the phone, he smiled to Angela and hugged her close.

"Papa said Dorothy was already calling the airline. They'll come in on Wednesday."

"Do you think her daughter will be upset?"

"I didn't ask, but they've been there for three weeks already. I think she'll understand. It is a wedding, after all," Mark said.

Any other time she and her mother set out shopping, Angela would be resigned to acquiesce. But something had changed. Who was she kidding? Everything had changed. Somehow Cathy was getting what she wanted—Angela married sooner than later. And Angela was getting what she wanted—a small gathering of close family and friends. And Florinda. And best of all she was marrying a man who was so good and genuine she wasn't sure if she would ever deserve him. They were both having their way without it costing the happiness of the other.

What stars could be aligned?

Or, rather, what trees were aligned?

After all, Caroline had chosen two trees.

"This is the place I was telling you about," her mom said.

One glance of the storefront and Angela moaned. "You said it was understated. Why is there valet parking?"

"You never said anything against that," Cathy said innocently, like what could be wrong with a dress shop that had valet parking?

"I didn't think I had to," Angela said.

Maybe this is where their shared dreams would come to an end. Maybe this would be the undoing of the entire event.

"Our definitions of *understated* may be vastly different," Angela said as they approached the doors. "My other conditions still stand, right? Nothing over the amount we discussed, nothing imported, and I have the final say."

"Of course you have the final say. You're the bride."

Again, Cathy's tone worried Angela. How did she get into fixes like this?

An hour and a half later, Angela was trying on her last dress and couldn't believe what she was about to tell her mother.

"I like them. I like them all."

"That's wonderful, dear, but you do have to choose one," Cathy said.

"I didn't think you could do it. I'm amazed."

"Do what? Find American-made, no hoop skirts, no taffeta? Honestly, those were easy requests. Now the no-train requirement was harder to handle, but mostly because I don't think a dress *is* a wedding dress unless it has a train. But this is your traditional mother talking. The Markum's daughter didn't have a train." Her voice trailed off.

"I meant I didn't think you could stay within a budget," Angela said, staring at the last dress.

"Oh, well, that. I can compromise when I need to."

Angela may have been too distracted by the way the dress accentuated parts of her body she didn't usually accentuate—but something in that comment raised her suspicion.

"What do you mean compromise?"

"This doesn't have to be the only dress you wear. I mean, should you and Mark decide to go through with another ceremony, like the wedding you were planning for the spring, I'd be more than happy to get you a real dress."

A real dress? What am I wearing, then?

"Mom." Angela turned to face her mother, and with all the intensity she could manage, she said, "We are only having one wedding. This is it. Not another one in a few months. Not another one in some grand hall. And not another dress. This week will be everything I've ever wanted."

Cathy was stunned. She took to arranging the skirt portion of Angela's dress. "This is lovely. It was just a suggestion. Of course you only need one ceremony." Her voice was flat.

"Please don't do this," Angela said quietly to her mother.

"Do what?" Cathy asked simply.

"Don't ruin it. I don't need a bigger, better, more expensive anything. Mark and the farm and you and Caroline and Florinda. I couldn't ask for anything more. No, I wouldn't ask for anything more because it is enough. I'm so full of love I don't need to try and fill it with more clothes or shoes or jewelry. Please be content with me. Let this be enough."

Cathy met Angela's eyes with a surprised but softened expression. "You are a beautiful bride. And I know you and Mark are going to be very happy."

That did it? Had she only known, she would have confessed her happiness much sooner.

"Have you chosen the one you like?" Cathy asked.

Angela eyed the dresses. *It's not about the dresses*, she thought. *But I still have to pick one.*

The dress took up much of the closet space in the master bedroom. She unzipped the plastic cover, allowing it to air out. She lifted the long lace sleeves away from the bodice.

Caroline walked in. "Are you going to try it on?" she asked excitedly.

"No, I was letting it breathe," Angela answered. "It fit when I tried it on. It will fit tomorrow. What about your dress? It's still on the hanger, right?"

Angela's phone rang. It was Dorothy calling from the airport in DC.

"Have you seen the news?" she asked.

"Not recently. What is it?" She instantly knew something was wrong, but she looked at Caroline, not wanting to alarm her.

"The weather. It's gotten worse," Dorothy said.

"I thought the storm wasn't as bad as they thought. We've had a fresh layer of snow but nothing like the blizzard they predicted."

Again, Angela kept her voice even as Caroline listened to every word.

"Our flight to Boston has been cancelled, as have many others. It's not the snow. We've been told Logan airport is closed due to the freezing rain. I'm so sorry, dear. We tried our hardest to be there with you."

"They don't have another flight? What about Providence?

What about that small airport in Worcester?" She couldn't contain her panic, not even for Caroline's sake. "What about the morning? Will they be resuming flights?"

Angela listened as Dorothy shared how many other passengers needed flights too. And how she and Papa were quite tired as they'd had a four-hour layover in Denver early that morning. And how very sorry she was. When Angela suggested they postpone the wedding, knowing that would mean Florinda would miss it—Dorothy insisted they go through with it.

"We'll celebrate when we get there, whenever that may be."

When she finished the call, she looked up at Caroline's face. It was full of questions.

"I don't think they'll make it," Angela said softly. "They want us to still have the wedding, but I'll talk to Mark. I can't imagine Papa not here with us, not here for him."

"You have to get married tomorrow. We picked out a love-match tree. And Papa said." Her lower lip quivered. "Papa and Dorothy need to be here."

Caroline ran from the room. Angela called after her, following her to the front of the farmhouse. "Come back. It will work out," she said. But could it?

Caroline had thrown on her coat, pulled on her boots, and was already off the porch. Angela grabbed her coat and headed out to find her daughter. The sun had set almost an hour ago, and except for a few of the lot lights, darkness had settled around them. She fought back tears, knowing they would only chap her cheeks if she let them fall. She had allowed herself all the excitement a bride-to-be should have, only in this moment to feel like they might have made a mistake. Papa and Dorothy were stranded in DC and short of a miracle, they wouldn't make it home in time.

She stopped in the slushy snow. Caroline was standing in between two trees, facing one with her back to Angela.

"It's Papa and Dorothy," Caroline said. "They have to be here. You know it, and I know it."

Angela strained to hear all of Caroline's words. Mark approached, jogging up to where she stood.

"What's going on?"

She put a finger to her lips for him to be quiet, then pointed.

"We need a wedding here one way or another." Caroline had become quiet after she'd spoken. She brushed the snow off a branch and held on to it.

"What's going on?" Mark whispered. "What's she doing?"

"Dorothy called. Their flight's canceled. Logan is closed. I'm so sorry, Mark. We can wait. It's not right for them to miss it."

"Is that what they said?"

Angela hesitated, watching Caroline. "Actually, they insisted we go through with it."

Mark stretched his arms out wide and then brought them together again, rubbing his hands together for warmth. "Would you be okay with that?"

"I am if you are," Angela said.

"Caroline," Mark called to her. "Let's go in. I want to marry your mom tomorrow, and I don't want anyone to get cold feet."

Caroline came running. "Do you think they'll make it home in time?"

"We hope so," Angela said.

CHAPTER 24

Mark stood near the decorated tree, adjusting his tuxedo. It fit fine, though it was a little tight through the shoulders. He pulled on his shirtsleeves to allow at least a half inch to show, as the man at the tux rental shop had told him.

The windows and fireplace mantel and any other fixtures Cathy had gotten her hands on were adorned with white roses, satin bows, and large pinecones. She had strings of lights from corner to corner. She'd insisted on white, padded chairs for the guests, a catered meal, and enough candles to survive a lengthy power outage. But Angela refused the horse-drawn carriage.

Not that any of the guests were paying much attention to the decorations or Mark's shirt cuffs. They were watching Angela.

He waited an extra moment, breathed deeply, and then turned to see her emerge from the bedroom walking, maybe floating, down the hall and into the dining room.

Her dark, curly hair was a stunning contrast against the white of her dress. Half of it had been left long and down her back, and half of it was pulled up on the sides and tucked back in a way that showed off her creamy cheeks.

A snow angel, Mark thought at first. *No, a snow queen.*

She moved effortlessly toward him across the living room and joined him by the tree. He remembered her first night on the farm, wanting to know her name. He thought of how he'd kissed her last Christmas Day and how he proposed on the night of the flood. And how she had accepted him as the keeper on their trip to the chasm. He thought of what their future might hold, and that led to one overriding thought that seemed to quiet all the others.

Don't mess this up.

Mark stood by her side, and the new, young pastor spoke and smiled a lot, which Mark thought he was doing to cover his nervousness. For some reason it put Mark at ease. If their pastor was anxious, he didn't have to be.

Suddenly the front door burst wide open, followed by a rush of cold air and the stomping of feet.

"Papa!" Caroline shouted.

"Dorothy!" Angela said, though not as loudly as Caroline. "You made it!" she said, rushing over to hug Dorothy.

"Looks like barely just," she said, unwrapping the scarf from her neck and shaking off some of the snow that had fallen on it. "What a stunning bride you are!"

"Didn't know what time the ceremony was. We got the last rental car they had on the lot and decided we didn't have anything to lose by giving the roads a try," Papa said.

Mark came and gave him a quick embrace.

"Please excuse our traveling clothes," Dorothy said.

"You're here. That's all that matters," Angela reassured them.

"I knew you'd make it. I knew it," Caroline said giving them each hugs.

"Don't let us stop the proceedings. Pastor Kenny is waiting."

With that, Mark and Angela returned to their places and the pastor gave a sigh of relief and wiped the sweat from his brow with his own handkerchief.

It looked to Mark like he was still nervous. Though Mark wasn't. He felt like he was in a dream—Angela standing beside him and saying "I do," and then him saying "I do," and then Caroline and Cathy hugging them and Papa being introduced to Gary.

Dorothy helped with the glasses, and Brett raised a toast. Florinda had brought a gift for them and insisted they open it right away. Angela peeled back the paper to reveal a set of hand-embroidered linens with an intricate floral design.

"Did you stitch these?" Angela asked. "They're beautiful."

"From my hands for your precious family," she said.

"This must have taken so much time," Mark said. Not that he knew too much about sewing, but Donna had taught him a thing or two. "Thank you."

"Time we spend loving—it's why we have time, no?" she said and gave them both hugs and cheek kisses.

Cathy was motioning to the caterer she'd brought that it was time for some dinner and insisting they sit at the table and eat.

After dinner, Mark took Angela by the hand and led her to *their* dance floor and motioned for Brett to turn the music on from inside the studio. Finally, Mark had a chance to be "alone" with Angela amid the bustle of people and food and music.

"You know the winter solstice is the shortest day of the year. But this one will live the longest in my memory. Thank you for wanting to spend four seasons with me and sharing what all our future seasons have in store. I love you, Mrs. Shafer."

"I love you," she replied, tightening her arms around his neck. Her eyes sparkled with tears. "Thank you for this room—and thank you for making room."

CHAPTER 25

Angela and Mark sat side by side on the couch. As he put his arms around her, she nestled into him.

"You can hardly tell that tree took a beating," Mark said.

"I was worried Caroline had gone overboard. I don't think you could fit one more ornament on it, but it is stunning." Angela looked to each branch, staring in awe at how it hardly looked like the sorrowful little tree from a few weeks ago.

A few weeks ago. That triggered more memories. When they'd cut down the tree, she had no idea her mother was bringing Florinda to Sutton. She had no idea they would be married before the holiday or that she'd be snuggling up to Mark on the couch on Christmas Eve while Papa and Dorothy were settling in at the house on Hickory.

"Now I'm feeling kind of sad we didn't put up a tree at my house."

"Why is that?" Mark asked.

"For Papa and Dorothy. I'm not sure it feels like a holiday over there," Angela said. "Maybe she's put up some decorations."

"I bet Papa isn't too worried about it," he said with a sly grin.

Angela smiled too. This had to be one of her favorite moments of the holiday every year. A quiet house, a festive tree.

All is calm. All is bright.

Mark stroked the side of her hand as he held it in his—a small motion, but it drew her attention. No ring. There was a pang of—what? Sadness? No, that wasn't it. Melancholy, perhaps. She'd told Mark not to buy a new ring. He'd said he would if it didn't turn up before March. They didn't know they'd be getting married on the winter solstice instead of the spring equinox.

But she'd had a feeling that it would turn up. As unlikely—no, as impossible—as it sounded, she had thought it would. She sat up and shook off the thought, not wanting anything to ruin this perfect moment.

"What is it? Are you cold?" Mark pulled her closer.

"I'm fine," she said.

"Is it safe to wrap some presents? She's been asleep about an hour."

"We *think* she's been asleep that long," Angela answered. "But yes, it should be safe."

She pulled the presents from the hall closet. Mark went to the office at the back of the farmhouse—the one room where Caroline never ventured—and rolled out the bike he'd managed to disguise with a green canvas cover he used for the lawnmower.

"I don't think she suspects a thing."

Angela sat cross-legged at the foot of the tree with a few presents spread out in front of her along with an assortment of wrapping paper, bows, and ribbon. Mark joined her. They whispered quietly as they worked, wondering what time Caroline might wake them up in the morning. Maybe she wouldn't even care about her presents since she'd already received her Christmas wish.

"She'll be pulling on her boots and begging to go see the trees," Mark said.

"And I'm good with that," Angela said. "I'll stay out there with her until my toes get cold, and then I'm coming back in."

"Good, because I'll be making breakfast."

"Since when do you cook?"

"I don't, but I can hope for a Christmas miracle, right?" he said, placing a wrapped present next to the village.

Angela laughed, but the melancholy returned at that word. "Mark, do you think . . . ? Never mind. We need to fill her stocking."

"What? Ask me."

"The trees. The miracle trees. Do they create love matches?"

"We're married, aren't we? The way I see it, we can say it was either the trees or your mother's calculated efforts."

Angela couldn't resist the laugh. "Let's call it the trees."

"Pretend you're not seeing me do this," Angela said. She went to the kitchen and returned with a stocking for Mark and put it under the tree.

"No fair," he said. "You didn't tell me we were filling stockings for each other."

"I don't need a stocking," Angela said.

Mark stood and reached for Angela. "Are we done?" he asked expectantly.

"Almost." She kissed him and then went about rearranging some of the presents and the village while Mark stood watching her.

She sat back on her heels and took one last look, excitement welling up inside her. A sparkle from the tree caught her eye. Of course, the entire tree sparkled, but this was a glimmer at the base of a branch next to the trunk. She knelt down and crawled closer to the tree, careful not to crush the mirror ice pond.

"Angela? What is it?"

She reached toward the glimmer. Something was lodged in the bark of the tree where the branch jutted from the trunk. It was cool to the touch.

"Is there something wrong with the tree?" Mark asked.

She was now on one knee and bracing herself with the other leg. She wobbled a bit as she used both hands to grasp the small, round, glittering . . .

"Mark, I'm trying to . . . there's a . . ."—she moved the branch and pulled it free—"a ring!"

Too stunned to speak, Angela collapsed to the floor. She turned the ring over and over. A diamond band. Some dirt in the channel, but sparkling and gold.

"Mark, could this be?"

"Let me see that." He said as he reverently took it from Angela's grasp and strained to see it in the light from the tree. After a moment he looked wide-eyed at Angela. "This is it. This is the ring. *The* ring! I don't know how it could be. It was in my pocket, and then the flood." He sat down on the sofa, and Angela sat next to him. He held the ring out where they both could see it.

"The water carried it to that tree," Angela whispered, as if it were too risky to say it louder.

"The tree Caroline chose. For the farmhouse."

"And for us," Angela said.

Mark took the underside of the shirt he wore and rubbed some of the dirt from it. Then he took Angela's hand and asked, "May I?"

She watched as the ring came to rest at the base of her finger. They hugged, and she might have cried, but not so much that she couldn't return the kiss Mark gave her.

"Your grandmother's ring—it's beautiful. Thank you," Angela said, resting her head on his chest.

"I didn't tell you?" Mark asked. "Wait, I never had the chance."

She lifted her head to see his face. Why the worry in his tone?

"It wasn't my grandmother's."

Angela gulped at that. "Your great-grandmother's, then?"

"It's the ring my Dad bought . . . to give to . . . Cathy."

"To my mom?" Angela stared at the sparkling band already resting on her ring finger. How was it possible? When would she stop being amazed at this life with Mark? It was like he'd given her a part of the past—her past, along with the promise for their future.

They held each other on the sofa for hours—hours they weren't counting—until they admitted they would need some sleep before Caroline came to wake them.

Angela found Mark crouched by the fireplace. When she stepped up behind him and put her hands on his shoulders, he stood and hugged her. Something she would never get tired of, she was sure.

She'd had this idea from the moment she'd woken up, but with Caroline and the trees and presents, she hadn't had time to tell Mark. She was also afraid he might not agree, but she needed to ask before Cathy arrived.

"You know how I was having trouble finding a gift for my mom?"

"Our mom," Mark teased.

"Right." That would take some getting used to, Angela

thought. "Last year, I don't know how Caroline knew, but she knew, and Cathy loved the music box. But this year I haven't been able to think of anything."

"I thought you said you found a photo album."

"Yes, a discount photo album. An empty one for her Europe pictures."

"I thought that was a great idea for the woman who has everything," Mark said.

Angela paused. This was harder than she thought it would be. The risk of offense felt greater than ever.

"She doesn't have everything, and there is something money can't buy her. Something I have."

Mark looked at her intently now. "Angela, the farm isn't for sale," he said it half-jokingly, half seriously.

Angela slid the diamond band off of her finger and held it up.

"You're sure this was the ring your father bought to give to my mother?"

Mark stared at the ring. "The appraiser said as much." He looked at her as another quiet moment passed. "You're talking about the ring."

Angela nodded, holding her breath.

"You want her to have the ring?" Mark asked.

"Only if it's okay with you. I love it. You know I love it. But when I woke up this morning, it was the first thing that came to my mind, how this amazing ring needs to be hers."

Mark smiled and nodded. "Of course. It's your ring now if you want your mom to have it. Of course . . ." he paused, "I don't have another ring, though."

She hugged him. "I know. And that's not what matters."

Angela planned that after dinner, when there was a quiet moment for the two of them, she'd give her mother the ring. But Papa and Dorothy had arrived a little early and Angela had gotten started in the kitchen preparing dinner. Cathy showed up and offered to help—yes, to help—with dinner. And Mark was not going to be left out. Caroline had started helping but then convinced Papa to take her on another tour of the trees.

She and Dorothy and Cathy and Mark were in the kitchen peeling potatoes and sautéing vegetables. As Angela reached for a serving bowl in front of Cathy, her mom grabbed her hand.

"What's this? You do have a ring!" She studied Angela's hand. "Very nice, Mark. Was this a Christmas present? What am I saying? It had to be."

Angela looked to Mark with raised eyebrows. Was now the right time? At the risk of delaying dinner, Angela began.

"Mom, here." She slid the band off and gave it to her mother, who thought perhaps Angela was giving it to her for closer inspection.

"You realize you've already gotten it dirty?" Cathy reached for a dishcloth to wipe it off.

"Mom, I was going to try and clean it and give it to you later."

"What do you mean, give it to me?"

"I want you to have it."

Papa and Dorothy looked confused at what she'd said, but no one was more bewildered than Cathy. "What are you talking about? Mark, what does she mean?"

"She means you can have it."

"For heaven's sake. Just because I asked you about the ring a few times." She shook her head and was handing the ring back to Angela as Mark continued.

"That was the ring we found in the box last year."

"I remember," she said.

"The ring my father bought for a girl he wanted to marry," Mark said softly.

Cathy gasped.

Dorothy started to weep. "Alberto, I need a handkerchief."

"For me?" Cathy said as the realization washed over her. "For me."

She and Angela and Mark moved to the front room by the fireplace. Cathy had been mostly speechless and stared at the ring for the better part of ten minutes. She finally looked to Mark and then to Angela. She reached for her daughter's hand and put the ring into it.

"This is yours. All yours. To know it was meant for me once is enough. More than enough. You've given me a gift, to find out that someone I thought had fooled me truly loved me. And to know that a part of that love story and that miracle continues with you. That's all I need."

Angela tiptoed away from Caroline's room after confirming she was asleep. With all the miles the nine-year-old had hiked with Papa around the trees, calling it her best Christmas Day ever, Angela suspected she was *sound* asleep.

The fire had dwindled to a few glowing embers. Mark sat on the couch facing the lighted tree. Angela joined him, sitting close enough that he could put his arm around her. She tucked her legs up under the blanket.

Christmas night always provided relief. The stress of the holiday was mostly over. Tonight she felt more than that. Peace and contentment and, yes—*joy*.

"Do you have any more pain in your leg?" she asked as she gently rested her hand on his knee.

"It's healed fine. Can hardly see the scar."

Mark lifted her hand and examined the ring. "Do you like it?"

"Of course I do!"

"Are you sure? Would you like a new ring?

She sat up to face him, not sure he could be serious. "Thank you for the offer, but don't you know what this means to me?"

He sat up a little straighter and shook his head.

"Every time I look at this ring I'm reminded of not one, not two, but more miracles than I can count. Maybe when the next one happens I won't be so surprised," she said as she twirled the band on her finger. "But you know what? Maybe I will."

"Why is that?" he asked, touching her cheek with his hand.

"The trees and you—this life and our love—will always be a glorious wonder to me."

The End

ACKNOWLEDGMENTS

Thank you to the readers of my first book, *The Christmas Tree Keeper*, who cared about the characters and story and asked for more. Their enthusiasm and confidence kept me going through countless rewrites and revisions.

I give sincere thanks to Anna DeStefano of Precision Editing Group. To Heidi Brockbank, Sabine Berlin, and Michele Preisendorf of Eschler Editing—the skilled editors who worked hard to help this story come to life. I am in awe of their expertise and wisdom.

I offer heartfelt thanks to Valerie and Peggy, my allies in the whirlwind, for their indispensable support. And to all of the fabulous members of ANWA, my writing group, for continued feedback and friendship.

To my beta readers and those who aided my research, for their vital insights: Cathy, Valerie, Peggy, Jorie, Sofia, and Spencer.

To Laura J. Miller for her gorgeous cover work and E. A. Smart III for another lovely and fitting illustration.

I owe the most gratitude to my family for their love and support. To Steven for tireless tech support. To Marissa for celebrating the milestones with me. To Lauren who, when I was so close to the finish line said, "You can do it, Mom." And to Grandma Johnson who advised, "The book could have a little more kissing."

And to my husband Steve, for making room, not just for a room full of books but for a girl who likes to write them.

ABOUT THE AUTHOR

Tamara Passey, author of the #1 Amazon bestseller, *The Christmas Tree Keeper: A Novel*, loves crafting a story. She was born and raised in Massachusetts around a large family, one that has served as inspiration for most of her writing. She was named Arizona Young Mother of the Year in 2013 and contributes marriage and family articles to FamilyShare.com. She loves most creative endeavors and when she isn't writing, you can find her reading, baking, or cross-stitching. She lives with her husband and children in Arizona.

Visit Tamara and sign up for her newsletter online at www.tamarapassey.com.

Made in the USA
Middletown, DE
08 September 2019